# *Whose Side Are You On?*

## ALAN GIBBONS

*Cascades* consultants:
*John Mannion*, former Head of English, London
*Sheena Davies*, Principal Teacher of English, Glasgow
*Adrian Jackson*, General English Advisor, West Sussex
*Geoff Fox*, Lecturer at the University of Exeter School of
    Education, and a National Curriculum Advisor
*Emily Rought-Brooks*, Head of English, London
*Antonia Sharpe*, English teacher, London

## Collins Cascades

*Other titles in the* **Collins** *Cascades series that you might enjoy:*

### Hangman
JULIA JARMAN

Toby is determined not to be Danny's friend at secondary school. But how far can he avoid being Danny's friend without becoming his enemy?
ISBN 000 710 696 3

### Blitz
ROBERT WESTALL

Short stories of heroism and horror from one of the best-loved children's authors.
ISBN 000 711 484 2

### Breaking the Rules
SANDRA GLOVER

Suzie's teacher is horrified when her most difficult pupil is sent to do work experience in an old people's home. But the residents take a different view.
ISBN 000 711 184 3

*For further information call 0870 0100442*
*fax 0141 306 3750*
*e-mail: Education@harpercollins.co.uk*
*website: www.CollinsEducation.com*

# ALAN GIBBONS

# *Whose Side Are You On?*

*To Clare and Joanne,*
*May you stay forever young*

Published by HarperCollins*Publishers*
77–85 Fulham Palace Rd, London, W6 8JB

First published in Great Britain in 1991 by J.M Dent & Sons Ltd. Reissued in
Dolphin Paperback 2000 by Orion Children's Books, a division of the Orion
Publishing Group Ltd. 5 Upper St Martin's Lane, London WC2H 9EA

ISBN 0 00 713 441 X

British Cataloguing in Publication Data
A catalogue record of this book is available from the British Library

Cover artwork by Stewart Lees (NB Illustration)
Cover design by Ken Vail Graphic Design, Cambridge.
Production by Katie Morris
Printed and bound in China by Imago.

Project Management by Charlie Evans
Commissioned by Domenica de Rosa

# CONTENTS

# CHAPTER ONE

# Whose Side Are You On?

'Mattie, we want a word with you.'

Mattie Jones didn't want a word with Tony Doran and Joe Clarke. He never, but never, wanted words with those two. Doran was full of little hatreds and prejudices. He was always putting other people down. If anybody made a mistake in class, you would be sure to hear Tony's cackling laughter. If someone was upset about something, he would be there, taunting them. As for Joey, for as long as he had been knocking about with Tony he had been Tony Doran, only with muscles. Yes, he was like Tony Doran crossed with a fighting dog, a rogue fighting dog.

Mattie stole a glance at the two boys. Tony had planted himself smack in front of Mattie. Joe was leaning against the wall, ready to step in Mattie's way if he tried to turn and run. The two boys who confronted Mattie were smiling, but coldly. They were smiling with the assurance that came of being the school hard-cases, the ones you didn't cross. And Mattie? He was as tense and ill at ease as Tony and Joe were aggressive and confident.

'I said, we want a word with you.'

The tone of Tony's voice was unmistakable. It was shrill and angry. Taking a deep breath, Mattie looked into Tony's face. He looked at the boy's pinched, sallow features. He detested the smirk which played on his lips, the hint of senseless cruelty which was always there.

'We don't talk to Pakis,' said Tony, 'and we don't like any of our own people talking to them either, do we, Joe?'

Mattie didn't speak. He didn't dare to. Out of the corner of his eye, he could see Joe grinning. He talked like Tony and he acted like Tony. 'The trouble is,' thought Mattie, 'he fights like a mad dog.'

Mattie had only tangled with Joe once. It was in a quick game of football one playtime. Mattie had complained about a tackle. He wished he hadn't. He winced at the memory of the grip of Joe's fingers on his arm. Now Joe gripped his arm again.

'No, we don't like any of that lot, and we don't like you hanging about with them,' Joe said. 'Take a look at yourself in the mirror some time, Mattie. You're white, same as us.'

'What are you talking about, lads?' asked Mattie weakly. He felt sick at the sound of his voice. It came out thin and reedy.

Mum was always telling him that using words like 'Paki' was stupid and wrong. She had always told Mattie never to call people names because of their colour, the way they looked, or the way they talked. Mattie did his best, but he never seemed to be able to live up to his mum's expectations. Today was no exception.

He wanted to stand up to Tony and Joe, but he couldn't. There were another half-dozen like them in the school, and Mattie felt alone and scared.

'You know what we're talking about. We're talking about you and this new Paki.'

Tony was pressing a finger into Mattie's chest, slowly but with menace. It didn't hurt, but it made Mattie uncomfortable.

'Do you mean Pravin?' he asked.

Tony and Joe said nothing.

'He's all right you know, Tony. Why don't you give him a chance?'

Tony's face twisted into a sneer. 'We don't give any of his sort a chance. He shouldn't be here in the first place. This is a white man's country. We're going to make sure he knows he isn't welcome. Know what we're going to do — '

The whistle went. Tony and Joe walked slowly over to the line, glancing back meaningfully at Mattie.

Mattie followed them miserably. Joanne Carthy saw the look on his face.

'What's up, Matt? Are those two giving you a bad time?'

Mattie nodded, then he added: 'Not me, exactly. They told me to stop talking to Pravin. Three guesses what they called him. They make me sick.'

Joanne wrinkled her nose. 'You should tell them where to get off, you know. Don't take any notice of them. What could they do to you anyway?'

Mattie knew that Joanne was right. She usually was. She was a cool customer, was Joanne Carthy. She made things happen around her. She took control. Life wasn't like that for Mattie. Things happened *to* him. They ran out of his control. Mattie was about to say that Tony and Joe could do just about anything to him they wanted, when Mrs Carroll called:

'Joanne, Mattie. Stop chattering now. Let's have a bit of quiet as we go into school.'

By dinner time, Mattie had almost forgotten about his run-in with Tony and Joe. They soon reminded him.

Mattie was standing on his own in the playground, watching a couple of teenagers riding their motor bikes up and down the road by the school. Mattie looked forward to the day when he could have his own motor bike. Sometimes his uncle Johnny took him to the scrambling. Mattie wasn't even that excited by the races. It was the bikes themselves he loved, the feel of them, the smell of them. Perhaps what attracted him most to the idea of owning a bike was the freedom it would give him. When there was any bother, Mattie had always taken to his heels. But if he had a bike! With a bike, he would be able to get away, well away, at the first sign of trouble. Tony Doran's sharp, sarcastic voice broke in on Mattie's daydream.

'I hope you've been thinking about what we told you, Mattie lad. Don't go soft on us.'

Mattie moved away and stood by the school gates. No matter what he did, trouble came looking for him. The two bikers were cruising up and down the road, laughing wildly.

Mattie wasn't laughing.

Just then, Pravin walked over. Standing by Mattie's side, he gazed after the bikes as they roared off in the direction of the river.

'Watching the bikes, Mattie? Do you fancy one? Our kid's got a Yamaha 250. I think he's mad. He's nearly smashed his knee up once already. He's got so much metal in his legs that he has to keep clear of magnets!'

He was talking quickly, directing his words at Mattie and deliberately turning his back on Tony and Joe. He was used to their antics.

Pravin spoke with a pronounced accent. He was born somewhere up north. His dad had worked in a mill, then he got the chance to retrain as an engineer. Now that he had a trade he travelled round the city, mending washing machines.

Mattie liked Pravin. He was blunt and open. You knew exactly where you were with him. Oh yes, he liked Pravin all right, but he wasn't too impressed with his timing this sunny Monday morning. Mattie was keenly aware of Tony Doran. Tony's presence set Mattie on edge. Why was he such a coward? He'd always avoided fights, especially with lads who were tougher than him. What's more, he felt torn in two by the advice his mother gave him. On the one hand, she told him that name-calling was wrong. On the other, she told him never, repeat NEVER, to get into fights. Fighting, she insisted, didn't solve anything.

'That sounds great,' thought Mattie. 'The trouble is, Mum, how do you deal with the likes of Tony and Joe *without* fighting?'

'Is something bothering you, Mattie?' asked Pravin.

'Yes — YOU.' Tony's voice cut in sharp, incisive. He had made a bee-line for Mattie and Pravin as soon as it became clear that Mattie wasn't going to ignore his friend. Tony paused until Joe and his other mate, Ian Miller, were standing either side of Pravin, then he said:

'Yes, there is something wrong. You. Now, off you pop, before we get annoyed. We're all British here, aren't we Mattie?'

'Do you want me to go, Mattie?' asked Pravin.

Mattie looked away. He felt as if he was shrinking bit by bit, as the other boys waited for an answer. What did they want from him? Why couldn't they let him be?

'Leave me alone, all of you!' shouted Mattie, and he pushed his way between Pravin and Ian Miller.

Tony called after him: 'It's time you decided whose side you're on, you know. Whose side are you on?'

Joanne caught up with Mattie as he half walked, half ran across the yard.

'Hang on, Mattie. Hang on, will you? Where are you off to in such a hurry?'

'It's Tony and his mates,' said Mattie. He had tears in his eyes. They were tears of fear, tears of anger, tears of frustration.

'Oh, those two again,' sighed Joanne. 'What is it this time?'

'The same as this morning,' said Mattie. 'They don't like me having anything to do with Pravin. Ian Miller was with them and you know what a head-case he is. They said that we're all British and that I should know whose side I'm on.'

Joanne frowned. 'If being British means being like them, then make me Dutch or Australian, or African, anything but British. Prav's as British as they come, anyway. Where do they think he comes from? You only have to listen to that accent of his. They haven't got a brain cell between them, that gang.'

Mattie didn't say a word.

Joanne gave him a dig in the ribs. 'But they're bigger than you, aren't they?'

Mattie nodded, then gave Joanne an embarrassed grin. They'd known each other since nursery, and she always had a pretty good idea of what he was thinking and feeling. Mattie had a soft spot for Joanne. If there was a drawback with her, it was that she was a bit of a smart Alec. She had an old head on young shoulders. Some of the teachers thought Joanne was too full of herself. Mrs Carroll once called her 'arrogant' because she wouldn't admit she was in the wrong. It wasn't just the teachers who thought she was a bit too pushy for her own good. Mattie's mum would always say: 'Ten! She's never ten years old. Ten going on thirty, more like!' Still, Mattie always defended her to his mum. It wasn't her self assurance that bothered him. It was the way she was always pushing him. He knew she was right, but he just wasn't ready for it.

For a few moments, the Carthy magic worked, but just as Mattie was feeling a bit better, all hell let loose.

Mattie and Joanne could hear shouting from the far side of the playground. They could see children hurrying across the yard to see what was going on. Jimmy Mason was pushing Tony Doran up against the railings. Pravin was standing toe to toe with Joe Clarke. Ian Miller was yelling at Pravin at the top of his voice. Jimmy Mason was a black boy from Class Six. Though he was younger than Tony, everybody knew that he could take care of himself. There was no love lost between Jimmy and his friends and Tony's crew. It wouldn't take much to turn the dislike into open warfare. Maybe it was what everyone had been waiting for.

'Just leave him alone, right,' snapped Jimmy. 'One more word and I'll burst you.'

'Get your filthy black hands off me,' screeched Tony. He was beside himself with anger. 'I'll have you!'

The words were tough enough, but the look on his face told another story. He wanted someone to rescue him before he had to back down.

'You and whose army?' sneered Jimmy. 'I'll see you any time, anywhere. Name the place, lad. Just name the place.'

It was Joe Clarke who named the time and place for the settling of accounts.

Six o'clock that evening at the Fleapit.

The Fleapit was a derelict cinema down by the river, where people played football, rode their bikes, or just sat about talking. Twenty years ago it had been a place to go when you had money in your pocket and you wanted a good time. Now it was somewhere to hang around when you had nothing to do and nothing to spend, and that went for most of the people round there. It had the look of a brick and concrete ghost town, littered with broken glass and wind-tossed rubbish. Graffiti covered the bleak walls and the boarded-up windows.

Mattie didn't go to the Fleapit much. He was a boy who liked to think that he had a future and the Fleapit was a dead-end if ever he'd seen one. No, the river was his sort of place. He enjoyed his solitary walks by the riverside. The river was a silent witness to everyone and everything that there ever was in the city, and Mattie loved it for that.

For a moment or two it looked as though nobody was going to wait until they got to the Fleapit. Emboldened by Joe and Ian, Tony pressed forward. Jimmy and Pravin stood their ground. Small groups of boys hung around, tempted to join in on both sides of the fight. Just as it looked as if the angry silence was about to end in kicks and punches, the deputy head, Mr Parr, hurried over.

'What's going on here? I think this is down to you, Tony. What have you got to say for yourself? What's going on?'

'Nothing, Mr Parr. Honest. We're just having a bit of a laugh, aren't we lads?'

Tony looked as if butter wouldn't melt in his mouth.

Mr Parr looked at the boys. 'Jimmy, Pravin, have you got anything to say?'

Jimmy and Prav shrugged their shoulders.

'Look, lads, I didn't like the look of it. I didn't like it one bit. One more incident, and you'll all be in hot water. Understand. UNDERSTAND?'

The five boys nodded, but neither they nor Mr Parr believed for a minute that anything had been settled.

The moment Mr Parr disappeared into school, Tony called out to Pravin and Jimmy: 'The Fleapit, tonight. Be there.'

Joanne gave Mattie a sidelong look.

'Oh, give me a break, Joanne. It's got nothing to do with me.'

'Hasn't it?' she asked.

'I just want to be left alone. I don't get involved in fights. It's stupid.'

The words tumbled automatically from Mattie's mouth, but even he didn't really believe them. He knew Joanne was right. Mattie could tell she was annoyed with him. Why couldn't he make *his* mind up and take a stand? There were two sides to Joanne's character. On the one hand, Mattie loved her sympathy and understanding. On the other, he really hated those high moral standards of hers!

'I'm not asking you to fight,' said Joanne. 'I just think you're letting Pravin down if you don't stick up for him. Prav didn't ask for any of this trouble. If all this turns into black against white, there are going to be an awful lot more scraps. You know a lot of people who could stand up to Doran and his mates. Somebody's got to.

You'd better make up your mind where you stand. The more of us tell Doran and his mates what we think of them, the better it will be for all of us. I'm going to be there. What about you? Whose side *are* you on?'

Mattie shook his head vigorously. 'You can leave me out of it. I don't want to know.'

Joanne stared at him.

'I don't want to know!' Mattie shouted.

What was the use of knowing who was in the right and what was the use in taking sides? Tony, Joe and Ian were the cocks of the school. Stand up to them, and it didn't matter how right you were, you'd just get your silly head kicked in.

Mattie felt hot. His head was pounding. He felt angry and frustrated and ashamed all at the same time.

Joanne tried to hold onto his arm, but he brushed her off.

'Mattie!' she cried, as he suddenly dashed across to the bicycle racks. He unfastened the chain on his push-bike and pedalled out of the gates and down the road. He could hear the dinner supervisor calling his name, but he didn't turn round, or slow down. He didn't care if he got into trouble. He couldn't bear another moment in school.

# CHAPTER TWO

# Heywood House

Mattie felt as if he was burning up. His collar rubbed against the back of his neck. His trousers were clinging to his knees. There was a patch of sweat on his shirt between his shoulder blades. His heart was pounding. The pulse-beat in his temples was so strong that he felt dizzy. 'I'm well out of it,' he thought, 'well out of it. Let them have their fights. It's got nothing to do with me.' Mattie wanted to escape; to be as far as he could from the school yard and quarrels and taking sides. He wanted to get away. He'd been pedalling furiously for five or ten minutes when he realized with a start that he was on the main road out of the city.

To his left, the river shimmered like beaten bronze. 'Seen it all before, haven't you?' said Mattie out loud. The road forked away from the riverside. Within ten minutes Mattie was riding past the large, detached houses of the city's southern suburbs. Already, he was in foreign territory. The breeze felt deliciously cool against his skin. The rushing air pressed against him, easing away the pain and anger. Mattie swung his bike out on the long, curving bend. He was feeling good now. Too good. His pleasure was interrupted by the loud burst of a horn. A lorry driver shook his fist.

'Young fool!' he yelled. 'Do you want to get yourself killed?'

Even the close call with a thundering lorry didn't disturb the sense of calm and pleasure which swept through Mattie. A railway line ran alongside the road just a few metres across the fields. The southbound train approached. Mattie threw caution to the winds and took up the challenge. He pedalled and pedalled until the train raced away into the far distance. Then he pulled over onto the grass verge, panting and laughing.

'Ah well, it was a good try,' he said. 'By the way, Mattie lad, did you know that talking to yourself is the first sign of insanity?'

It was then that thoughts of Tony and Pravin and the others came flooding back. He didn't want to think about them, but he couldn't help it. He stopped laughing, but even the memory of their taunts couldn't completely crush his new-found high spirits.

Mattie set off again, riding more slowly now, but still cheerful and free. He rode on, putting miles between himself and the city. He reached the top of a long hill. Below him on one side lay the vast sprawl of the city, oppressive with its pent up anger and its conflicts. Ahead of him stretched fields and woods which seemed to blaze with green fire. The whole countryside was breathing slowly and easily.

Mattie free-wheeled down the hill. He had no idea how far he wanted to follow the road. He was intoxicated by the endless expanse stretching ahead of him. It promised a new world, maybe even a better one. Anything or anywhere which was familiar seemed hostile. The grim, red-brick walls around the school were like prison walls. Inside them you were caged, hemmed in. Conflicts simmered on and on. They stewed. They fermented. You were drawn deeper and deeper into them. Here, in the open countryside, there was no end to the newness of the world. It seemed to go on forever, Mattie was free and not just free of Tony and Joe. He was free of Mum and Joanne and Mrs Carroll and anyone else who wanted him to be different.

'If they could see me now!' he muttered.

He took a sharp bend and found himself facing a gateway. A stone pillar stood on each side. There was a coat of arms carved into each one, but time and vandals had worn and chipped away the details. The iron gates were hanging off their hinges. Beyond the gates stretched a long, straight drive, bordered by tall poplar trees which swayed in the summer breeze. Mattie couldn't see what lay at the far end of the drive. The poplars closed in the distance in a green, shimmering haze.

'Oh well, in for a penny, in for a pound,' Mattie said to himself.

It was the first time he had skived off school. Ever! Now he was determined to follow the drive to the very end, no matter where it led.

As Mattie rode along the drive, the sun flickered behind the poplars. Bars of light alternated with bars of shade. Mattie felt as if he was travelling downwards, rather than forwards. He went on riding down, down into the mystery which was drawing him on.

He saw his journey's end first as a fleck of reddish brown amidst the blanket of green. It grew into a solid block of that same reddish brown. Then Mattie began to make out details. There were windows, doors, towers, paths and gardens half-hidden by undergrowth. It was a house, vast, rambling, long abandoned. Mattie's heart turned over at the sight of it. There was something about it which was not quite real. It was a house all right, a thing of brick and mortar, yet it seemed to breathe, and shift, and alter as he looked at it. It was as if it was rolling on an invisible sea.

Mattie propped up his bike against the wall of the house. 'Well, that's real enough,' he thought. He shielded his eyes against the strong sunlight and scanned the boarded-up windows and doors of the large building. The frames were blackened. They had been scorched by a searing heat.

He stepped back a little and tripped over something. It was a 'For Sale' sign. It lay splintered on the ground. A single glance told Mattie that the house had lain empty and forgotten for many years. It had once been consumed by fire. Unlike the phoenix, it had never risen again. As he walked around the outside of the house, he realized he was treading softly and holding his breath. He wasn't quite sure why. Was it because he might be trespassing, or because the house was in some way special?

At the back of the house, Mattie discovered that one of the boards covering a small casement window was loose. It was just above his head. He searched for something to stand on and found an old barrel. By climbing up on the barrel, he was able to reach the window. Its frame too was smoke-blackened. He tugged at the board. It was rotten, and disintegrated in his hands. Mattie soon freed the rusty window-catch.

He hauled himself shakily up to the window and prepared to spring down. As he braced himself for the drop something burst from the gloom inside the house. Mattie felt beating wings brush against his face, then he lost his balance.

'No!' he cried.

When he opened his eyes he could feel blood trickling down his lashes. He had an idea that he had been knocked out for a moment or two, maybe longer. Mattie pulled out his handkerchief and mopped at the blood. The bleeding stopped. He looked about him. To his surprise, he could see sunlight pouring through the windows into a grand, beautifully furnished hall. It didn't make sense. Mattie expected to see dusty, forgotten rooms. He expected to see the sky through charred and broken rafters, and birds and animals making their homes in the crumbling brickwork.

Instead, he stood marvelling at a sumptuously decorated house.

Mattie stole across the thickly-carpeted floor. He had that same feeling of awe that he had experienced outside. He ran his fingers over polished wooden sideboards and cabinets. There wasn't a trace of dust anywhere, not a speck! Stranger still, it smelt sweet, as if it had been recently polished. He looked up. There, on every wall, in their dozens, hung oil paintings. There were so many that hardly a space was uncovered.

Mattie gave a low whistle and exclaimed: 'These must be worth a bit!'

He took in his surroundings. The more he saw of the furnishings, and the more the impressions of wealth crowded in on him, the less real it all felt. Everything he saw looked like part of a great puzzle, but the very pieces which should have held it together and made sense of it were missing.

Mattie examined the paintings. In one picture he saw a man on horseback riding with the hounds. In another there was a merchant logging goods on the quayside. Further along, he saw a portrait of two children, dressed in satins and velvets, cuddling their pet spaniel. Toys and belongings were littered carelessly on the ground next to them. There were paintings which showed various people, obviously well-to-do, involved in good works; laying the foundations of a church or a hospital, giving parcels of food to the poor. He saw the faces of men and women of all ages. Their eyes observed him coolly. What struck Mattie was how confident they looked, as it they hadn't a care in the world.

'As if they owned it,' he thought.

The men stood with their arms crossed over their chests, or with one hand resting on a hip. The older ones were plump and red-faced.

The look in the eyes of one reminded him of Tony Doran. Behind the calm, still gaze lay the hint of a cruel, mocking smile. Mattie read a small, oval metal plate on the frame. It bore the name Samuel Heywood. His portrait dominated the hall. Next to this picture was one which gave Mattie the creeps. A pale woman with creamy-white skin, a little older than his mum, stared haughtily at him. At her feet crouched a young black boy. The boy was dressed in a colourful, exotic costume. He wore a turban. The woman was resting a hand on the boy's head.

'She's patting him on the head like a little dog,' murmured Mattie. 'He's her pet.' His eyes scanned the plate on this picture: Victoria Heywood with Negro slave-child.

Mattie turned abruptly from the paintings and walked

26

along the hall until he came to a broad staircase. Slowly he climbed the stairs. From time to time he stopped. 'I don't get this,' he thought.

He paused on the landing.

Whether it made sense or not, it was all around him, as solid as he was. Mattie looked up, down and around. He thought of the tiny, second-floor flat where he lived with his mum. You could fit the whole place in this house, fifty or a hundred times over! Mattie examined a new painting which hung above the stairwell. It showed a sailing ship approaching the shores of some tropical land. Mattie couldn't understand what these pictures were doing here. They looked as if they were worth a fortune. This was supposed to be an abandoned house, wasn't it? And from the outside it looked as if it had been gutted by fire.

Now, Mattie didn't know much about old houses, but he did know that you shouldn't find the inside of an abandoned one looking like Harrods.

It was then that he discovered the biggest painting yet.

It covered most of the section of wall between two long windows, a little way along the landing from the top of the stairs. Two white men were standing either side of a black man. One of them was buying something. The other was happily pocketing the proceeds of the sale. Mattie peered at the expression on the face of the black man. It was grim. His near-nakedness contrasted with the well-dressed indifference of the two white men. He was for sale.

While Mattie was running his eyes over the painting, he caught sight of something moving through the window to his left. He couldn't explain what he saw. Instead of the weeds and tangled brambles, the broken timber and the litter he had seen on the way in, landscaped gardens stretched below him. They were laid out perfectly. And strolling casually along the gravel path were a man and woman in the same period dress as some of the figures in the paintings. Ahead of the couple ran two children. Mattie's heart raced. He pressed a hand to his forehead. It was damp with sweat. As he tried to make sense of the house, the gardens, the people below, a voice broke into his thoughts.

'Who are you? What are you doing at that window?'

Mattie spun round to find himself face to face with a stout woman, maybe forty years old. She was wearing a dark, plain dress, with long skirts. A bundle of keys hung from her belt.

Mattie's throat was dry. He opened his mouth to speak, but there was no sound.

The woman lost her patience: 'I'm going for the men. They'll shake your tongue loose for you, see if they don't. Coming into the master's house without an invitation! Oh, you're going to live to regret your impudence.' She was talking quickly.

She might be spitting fire, but she was quite unnerved by the strange figure standing in front of her.

Mattie looked from the housekeeper to the group in the garden; the world turned upside-down. The man and woman were staring up at him, their attention drawn to the upstairs window by the housekeeper's raised voice. Mattie recognized them with a shudder. They were the two people from the portraits: Samuel and Victoria Heywood.

Mattie felt as if he was being pulled by some strange force towards the garden. He stumbled dizzily. The two faces seemed to rush up at him, twisted and angry. He reeled against the wall. He felt as if the whole place was slipping and sliding, falling away before his eyes. He was weak and afraid. He lurched along the landing and plunged through the first door he came across. Harsh voices rose from the hall.

'There! He went in there!'

Mattie heard the sound of running feet. The room he entered was bright and lavishly furnished like the rest of the house. Mattie took in the furniture, the curtains, the paintings at a glance. The door handle began to turn. An awful thought struck him. There was no way out! He backed away from the door and looked around feverishly for somewhere to hide. Suddenly the room blurred in front of him. He put out a hand to steady himself, and felt the rough texture of an oil painting beneath his palms. This one took up the whole wall.

It showed a vast field of tall, green plants, being cut by tiny black figures. Palm trees bordered the field. The plate on the frame read Heywood Plantation, Jamaica.

The door began to open.

Mattie threw himself against the painting as though he thought those palm trees might hide him. Suddenly the entire house appeared to be falling away from him, dissolving into space. As he scrambled desperately, he no longer felt the canvas of the painting. In its place he felt water running through his fingers. Mattie tumbled forwards. The sunlight of the room faded, giving way to a dim light and the sound and feel of rushing water.

# CHAPTER THREE

# Runner

Mattie was falling for a long time, but in slow motion, as if in a dream. Ice-cold water ran over his face, his arms, his shoulders. He fell and fell. Without quite knowing why, he counted. He reached thirty before tumbling onto a greasy, moss-covered floor. He didn't feel any shock as he landed.

Raising himself slowly, first to his knees, then to his feet, Mattie turned. Where had he fallen *from*? And where was he? It looked like some sort of cellar. He scanned the wall of rock in front of him. It was moist and dark, worn smooth by the water which fell from a ledge above his head. As his eyes got used to the pale, greenish light, he could see that the wall was made of large slabs, resting against one another. Between the slabs there ran narrow cracks which sank into the wall. He reached through the water and into the nearest crack. Edging deeper into the opening in the rock, he managed to squeeze inside.

He couldn't see any way back yet, and he didn't really want to find one. Those people, whoever they were, would be waiting for him. He drew back, through the waterfall, and into the cellar. If he could discover another way out he might be able to find his bike and pedal back to town as fast as he could. He didn't know what it was he had seen. He didn't want to know. He just wanted to get away from this place. Mattie edged along the slippery stone ledge which led away from the running water. The light was still too gloomy to see very much. He had to feel his way out. Now and then, he touched things which really should not be in anybody's cellar.

For all the world, he felt as though he was brushing against the thick matted roots of plants. Then there were tiny creatures which felt like spiders or even shellfish and which scuttled away from the touch.

Mattie groped his way forward. Suddenly, his feet slipped from beneath him. A jet of water flipped him up into the air, and down again into a shallow pool. He stood up. The water in the pool reached his ankles, covering his trainers completely. His best trainers! He would usually have gone mad, but not now.

High above his head there was an enormous ceiling, carved out of rock. This was no cellar. It was a natural cave. There were bats hanging in rows from the roof of the cavern – huge bats, the sort you only saw on wildlife programmes on TV. Birds circled in their hundreds, chirping wildly. Ahead of him, Mattie could see the mouth of the cave. Sunlight flooded through the opening, filtering through trees and bushes which were quite different to any Mattie had seen.

'You should have stayed in school, Mattie lad,' he said, deliberately letting his voice break the silence. He was glad of its sound.

'Talk about out of the frying-pan and into the fire!'

Mattie often had little conversations with himself. Mrs Carroll was always teasing him about it. These little one-to-ones usually helped. Even so, he was on the brink of tears, or was it blind panic? He hadn't felt like this for years, not since he had lost his mother in a department store when he was a toddler, or since his dad had walked out one Boxing Day and not come back.

Mattie toyed with the idea of going back to the opening behind the waterfall, and the possibility of finding a way back. He wondered what the time was.

He glanced at his watch: one thirty. It had been one thirty when he recovered from his fall in the house. It was one thirty when he saw the couple in the garden. 'I must have broken it,' thought Mattie. 'My divers' watch, too. What a day! First it's a load of hassle in the playgound, then some freaks in period costume, then a pair of soggy trainers, now a broken watch.'

He had never felt so lost in his life. This place was unlike anywhere else he'd ever been. It shifted and changed at will. He had lost all idea of time. Mattie looked into the dark depths of the cave, then at its mouth. It was time to make a decision. He waded through the shallow water and squelched up on to the carpet of moss near the mouth of the cave. For better or for worse, he had to see what he had got himself into.

He looked out on a world he did not know. Palms rippled in a strong breeze. Other trees made up dense woodland. Beyond the thickly-wooded slopes which stretched below the cave, beyond a barrier of rock, Mattie could make out the sea. It was as clear and dazzling and blue as any island paradise in the glossy holiday brochures that his mum sometimes brought home – just to look at. Mattie sat down, hugging his knees into his chest. Weren't you supposed to click your fingers and say: 'I want to go home, I want to go home'?

Something like that. But no genie appeared to obey his summons.

Mattie sat for what seemed like hours. So much had happened to him, his head was spinning. He looked at his watch again. One thirty. Still broken. He saw a parrot in a tree, cleaning its feathers with its beak. The parrot took no notice of him.

Mattie decided to have his own clean-up. Why be outdone by a parrot? First, he emptied his pockets. He didn't find very much – a pen top, sixteen pence in loose change, an elastic band, a note for his mum about gala day. Then he took a look at himself. He was filthy. Though his clothes were drying quickly in the breeze, they were creased and dirty and covered in bits of leaf, wood shavings and mud. Mattie glanced at the coins in his hand. He read the dates: 1988, 1990, 1991. They didn't seem to make much sense – just numbers.

Mattie raised his head and squinted in the sunlight. He shaded his eyes with his hand and began to see details he had missed. There, in the bay, a large, three-masted sailing ship lay at anchor. It flew the red ensign. Mattie couldn't be sure, but he sensed that this was the ship he had seen in the painting in Heywood House. Mattie was no longer surprised by any of this. There is a limit to anything.

'It must have something to do with that house,' he thought. 'Everything is tied up with that house.'

Mattie was about to go back into the cave. 'I may as well take my chances with the house as get myself

34

deeper into trouble here,' he decided, when suddenly he was interrupted.

Somebody was running through the trees. A slim black figure flickered in and out behind the tree trunks. It was a boy. He was racing on long, lean limbs, and quick, nimble feet. A moment later, he began to climb the hillside, digging his bare feet into the earth to push himself up the steep slope. The boy was unaware of Mattie.

Mattie didn't know whether to speak, or to leave well alone. In the end he just watched. He could hear the boy panting. He could see his eyes. Mattie knew the expression on the boy's face well enough. He was afraid, and Mattie soon saw the cause of the boy's fear. Two men were chasing him. They were dressed in white shirts and trousers, tied at the waist with red sashes. In their hands, both men carried muskets. They moved slowly and were more clumsy than the boy, but they were close enough to use their muskets if they got a clear view of him.

'It's a runaway all right, a young 'un,' shouted one of the men. 'Keep your eyes peeled, John. He's in there somewhere.'

'Do you know which one it is?' called the second man.

'No, I didn't get a good look at him, but he's one of ours all right. He's got our brand mark on his shoulder.'

The boy was lying low in a thicket, panting with fright, but desperately trying not to make any sound which might give him away. Mattie had a good view of hunter and hunted. He was in an excellent position to guide the boy to the safety of the cave.

'If I just crawled through the undergrowth,' he thought, 'I could show him how to escape.'

He didn't dare. He feared that either he would give

himself away, or he would scare the boy and expose both of them to the armed men.

Meanwhile the two men were working their way up the hillside. One of them had slung his musket over his shoulder and was hacking away at the undergrowth with a machete. With each broad sweep of the blade he laid low a swathe of grass and creepers. The men were drawing closer to the boy's hiding place. Mattie had to act. There was nothing else for it.

He slipped onto his stomach, and pulled himself forward on his elbows. When he was almost level with the boy, he gave two little taps on a tree trunk with one of his coins. The boy turned. His eyes widened.

'Don't cry out, just don't cry out,' pleaded Mattie inwardly. He pressed a finger to his lips, then glanced in the direction of the concealed cave entrance. The boy followed the direction of Mattie's eyes, then crawled after him.

Mattie knew it was a matter of a few strides to the cave. On your stomach, it took an age to cover those few metres. Mattie looked up to check the whereabouts of the men. To his horror, one of them was standing astride the path to the cave. Mattie shrank back, and stretched out his hand to stop the runaway boy behind him. His fingers touched the boy's shoulder. The second man caught up with the one called John. Mattie could hear them breathing. The boys had no alternative but to retreat down the slope. They wriggled and slithered their way down the hillside. The hunters were pacing back and forth in front of the cave, lashing the undergrowth furiously.

'When I catch the wretch, I'll take the skin off his back,' snapped John.

'Don't waste your breath. What's one slave, when

there'll be hundreds more on the next ship?'

'I'll tell you what one escaped slave is. It's proof to them all that escape is possible. When we find him we'll make an example of him. It's the only rule they understand.'

Mattie looked at his companion. The boy didn't understand any of the discussion deciding his fate taking place on the hillside. He was more interested in reaching the thickest part of the woodland a few metres down the slope. Mattie followed him as he ran, crouching low, into the woods.

After a few moments, the dappled light of the woods gave way to the bright sunlight of open ground. In the distance stretched fields planted with tall, green shoots.

The boys stopped at the last line of trees. The runaway whispered something. Mattie didn't understand a word. The boy carried on talking. Bit by bit, Mattie began to pick up the odd word here and there. Soon, the boy's talk became perfectly clear. In normal times, this alone would have surprised Mattie, but these weren't normal times. If apparently burned out and derelict houses could turn out to be fully-furnished, and pictures could hide a whole forest, why shouldn't he learn a new language in thirty seconds? Mattie had made his mind up to take everything in his stride. Even if a tree trunk leaned over for a chat, he wouldn't have been *that* surprised!

'Why did you help me?' asked the boy.

'They were after you,' said Mattie. 'I thought they might hurt you.'

'But you're like them.'

Mattie was about to protest: 'Oh no, I'm not. I'm a runner like you.' Then he understood. Perhaps the boy had *never* been helped by anybody with a white skin. Perhaps they were all like those two on the hillside.

Mattie pointed to his heart and said: 'Not in here I'm not.'

The boy smiled. He placed his own hand on Mattie's chest. 'You have a good heart.' Then he added: 'Did they beat you?'

'Beat me?'

'Your head.'

Mattie had forgotten the wound on his forehead. He raised his fingers to his brow. It was sticky with dried blood.

'No', he said, 'they didn't do it. I fell.'

The boy turned towards the men on the hill. 'We can't stay here. The overseers will be returning this way. Come with me.'

Mattie was anxious. Where to? He didn't know anything about this place. He didn't belong here.

'I can't. I've got to go home,' he stammered.

'Where is your home?' asked the boy. 'Did you come on the ship?'

Mattie couldn't find the words. He must have looked confused and worried. The boy said nothing for a moment or two, then he hissed: 'Come.'

Mens' voices were approaching. Mattie remembered the muskets and the machete.

He followed.

# CHAPTER FOUR

# Slaves

'Stay here, and don't move. I must get back to the cane field before Burns notices. I'll be back for you after work is done.'

'Cane,' thought Mattie, 'Of course, it's sugar cane.'

Mattie crouched obediently among the bushes on the edge of the field. The sugar cane rose on tough, bamboo-like stalks. The green leaves rippled in a freshening wind. The canes towered above the heads of the men and women who were cutting them. The labourers were black. They were being supervised by a single white man. He was stocky and bearded and was leaning against a cart on the far side of the field. He was tapping his leg with a thick, heavy whip. Poking out above the side of the cart were the barrels of two muskets. As Mattie viewed the scene, two words came into his head: work and punishment.

Work came in the shape of the black man, punishment in the shape of the white man. Mattie suddenly realized what he was witnessing: slavery.

The young boy he had met by the cave slipped unnoticed among the cutters. He touched the elbow of a tall, well-built man. The man checked on the overseer, then bent quickly to hear the boy's whispered words. He seemed to freeze for a moment, staring down with an expression of disbelief. He worked on steadily for about a minute, then looked over in Mattie's direction.

Mattie dropped his eyes. He knew that his presence must be putting these people in danger. The thought of running flashed through his mind, but the arrival of the two men from the hill closed off that route.

The hunters exchanged words with the man by the cart, then the bearded man called: 'Ebo Jack!'

The tall man who had been informed of Mattie's presence stiffened at the name. He barely disguised his resentment of the overseer's voice. Straightening slowly, he turned towards the voice.

'Yes, Mr Burns.'

'I hear that one of this gang has been trying to run. Do you know anything about it?'

'No, Mr Burns. We have been here all the time, all of us. You know that.'

Burns scratched his beard with the whipstock. He looked annoyed that the slave hadn't replied more respectfully to him. He strode over to the man he had called Ebo Jack, and drew the whipstock slowly over the labourer's face.

'You wouldn't be telling me a tale now, would you, Jack? You know the price.'

'Yes, Mr Burns.' The black man stared steadily into

Burns' eyes.

All the while they were talking, the cutters had gone on working. They gave no sign of taking any interest in the conversation, but Mattie knew they were listening. He had seen their eyes meeting, little gestures passing from slave to slave. It was their secret, hidden language of defiance.

Burns turned his attention to the slaves. Heads bowed as he returned to the cart. He cracked the whip down hard on the side of the cart. He wasn't happy with the way Ebo Jack had answered him.

'Get on with your work, then,' he snapped. 'You won't cut cane standing there with your mouth open.'

The work looked back-breaking. It went on, hour after hour, without respite. There were about fifty men, women and children working in the field. They were all dressed in the same coarse linen clothing. Most were dressed in white, though there was the occasional striped shirt or dress. The men wore breeches, the women loose, shapeless dresses. Some wore turbans or bandanas as protection against the sun. A group in the distance were occupied digging ditches with picks and spades in the sun-baked soil. Others were felling canes, then stripping away the leaves with knives or machetes.

Across the waving ocean of sugar cane, Mattie could just make out other gangs working. One of the slaves was wearing a broad, iron collar which forced his head up into a position which afforded him no comfort. From time to time he paused to rub at his neck where the metal chafed against his skin. Children younger than Mattie were hurrying back and forth loading the canes into the cart.

Mattie picked up a piece of cane and turned it over in his fingers. It ought to be a thing of beauty. Instead, it was the living chain which bound the slaves to their labour.

A strange sound interrupted Mattie's thoughts. It was like a strangled bugle call. Burns was blowing a large pink-and-white conch shell. Some of the slaves dropped gratefully to the ground. Others walked slowly over to the cart from which John had begun to ladle measures of water from a barrel.

The bush, behind which Mattie was sheltering, shook. A small, black-skinned hand poked through, holding out a cup of water. Mattie hesitated then reached out for it.

'Drink quickly and hand back the cup to me. You mustn't be found, Irishman.'

IRISHMAN? Mattie opened his mouth to ask what on earth that was supposed to mean, but the boy shook his head. Too dangerous.

The shell-bugle sounded again. Cups were returned to the cart and the labour recommenced. In the sweltering heat, arms were raised, arms fell. Long knives cut cane. Cane fell. Then the whole movement began again. Swing, swish, cut. Swing, swish, cut. The boy trotted back and forth like the other children, carrying armfuls of cane. At intervals, the cart rolled off in the direction of a half-hidden jumble of buildings some distance down a rough track.

Dusk gathered at last over the rich, green land. With the fading light came a strengthening breeze. Mattie shivered. He felt cold and tired. His mind was in a spin. What was he doing in this history-book world anyway? He couldn't resist the temptation of peering through the leaves of the bush. He saw that the cart was on the move. Burns and the other two men were taking a ride, their legs hanging over the side of the cart. They rested their muskets and whips on their laps, and glanced from time to time at the weary slaves who were following them. The boy and Ebo Jack were the last to leave the cane field.

Burns made ready to jump down from the cart, bellowing: 'You two. Get a move on!'

Mattie's throat tightened.

'We're coming now, Mr Burns,' called Ebo Jack, sliding his knife under a pile of cane leaves. 'It's my bill. I dropped it here somewhere. I should find it in a moment.'

As Ebo Jack crouched, pretending to look for his bill knife, he nudged the boy, who edged closer to Mattie's hiding-place.

'Stay there until you can follow without being seen. There will be a square of cottages. Find yourself a new hiding place nearby, and we will come and find you. Remember, Irishman, be careful. Oh, Irishman . . .'

'Yes?' whispered Mattie.

'I trust you, but if you're a spy, the others will cut your throat.'

Mattie frowned, but said nothing.

Burns was barking out orders: 'Move, I said. Run! Come on, you idlers. You're keeping me from my grog. I want you in your cottages before the moon comes up.'

Ebo Jack glanced sideways. The boy nodded.

'I've found it, Mr Burns.' He and the boy picked up their feet and loped after the cart.

Mattie stepped carefully as he made his way towards the little village of wood and thatch houses. The cane fields surrounded the slave dwellings like a vast, green sea. Above the cane stalks rose banana trees whose leaves, as broad and long as a child, waved lazily in the freshening breeze. The huts were maybe six metres long, and half as wide. They were simple in construction and windowless.

Mattie crept forward under cover of the thickening dusk until he reached a grove of orange trees. He took shelter there, and scanned the scene before him. Cottages indeed! How could Burns call these hovels cottages? The cluster of slave quarters stood cheek by jowl next to patches of land which grew the odd crop. A few chickens scratched half-heartedly in the dirt.

Beyond the 'village' Mattie could see a large, stone-walled building. It was shaped like the keep of a castle. Through the open door came a fiery glow, doubly hellish against the darkness. Sheds and workshops stood nearby. Steam rose from large pots and the sweet smell of sugar and the acrid smell of burning wood hung on the air. Beyond these buildings, pale and elegant in contrast to the rest of the estate, stood a large, wooden house with open balconies and verandahs where shadowy figures sat and talked. The darkness shrouded their faces, but Mattie knew they were not slaves.

Some minutes passed. Mattie was trying desperately to fight back his tiredness. The faces of Pravin, Tony Doran, Burns and the slaves swam before his eyes. It was a losing battle. Afraid as he was of being found, he couldn't keep his eyes open a moment longer. By the time the boy was able to steal out of his cottage, Mattie was already dozing.

'Hey, hey, wake up.' said the boy, 'you can come into our cottage. Stay low.'

Mattie tried to rouse himself, but dragged his feet as he followed the boy into a cottage. The only light in the hut streamed in through the open door from the brilliant new moon. A thin wooden partition divided the hut into two rooms. There were five people in the room Mattie entered, and they were all sitting on the beaten earth floor. Ebo Jack squatted next to a woman Mattie took to be his wife. She was cradling a baby in her arms. A little girl was playing with smooth pebbles in the middle of the room, and in the corner, with his arms resting on his knees, sat a big, heavily muscled man. He was almost lost in the darkness, except for his eyes which burned. He alone did not turn his head as Mattie and the boy entered.

Ebo Jack spoke: 'Kota, keep a look out for Burns and his men. They might patrol to check on the new shipment of field workers.'

Kota sat in the doorway, looking out across the square. Ebo Jack pointed at Mattie. 'You, come here by me.'

Mattie did as he was told. He stood nervously, staring down at the floor. Ebo Jack questioned him. Did he come on the ship? Had he ever been in the big house? Was he from the hills? Did he know the Irishman?

That again! Mattie shook his head. No, he didn't know the Irishman.

'Then who are you? Where are you from? Do you know Burns?'

Mattie looked into Ebo Jack's eyes. He couldn't detect any hint of the man's feelings towards him. He began to pour out a stream of words: 'My name is Mattie. I'm not from here, and I'm not a spy. Please, Ebo Jack, don't cut my throat . . .'

Ebo Jack lifted his hand. He gave the glimmer of a smile as he said: 'Kota has spoken for you. I trust him. You've had plenty of opportunity to betray us. You're not one of them, but what you are . . .' He looked at Mattie's clothes. 'What you are, I cannot guess.'

Mattie was relieved and grateful.

Ebo Jack spoke again: 'Now, listen to me. Listen carefully and never forget what I tell you. You must never call us by the names the master gave us. I am Cuffee. The slaveholder gave me the name of Ebo Jack. It is something they like to laugh about. It is their mark upon me. I must bear it in the fields, but I will not bear it in these walls. Here, I am a free man, I go by my own name. Do you understand?'

Mattie nodded. He understood all right! Cuffee rested his hand on Mattie's shoulder. 'You helped Kota today. We owe you our thanks.' He paused and ran a hand over his brow. 'If only ...' He shook his head slowly. 'This is a bad time to have a stranger among us. There are dozens of unseasoned workers in the fields, newly-arrived from Africa.'

The woman raised a long finger to her lips. Cuffee nodded.

Mattie watched the exchange, then asked: 'Kota, why *were* you running?'

Kota made as if to speak, but the woman's eyes silenced him. Mattie sat silently, at the heart of an invisible web of secret communications.

At last he plucked up the courage to speak: 'I want to explain where I came from. At least, I want to try. I don't really understand it myself. It was like, well, like magic. One moment, I was in my own time, the next I was here, in yours. What year is this? Is it the eighteenth century? The seventeenth?'

Mattie blushed. He expected his explanation to be ridiculed. 'I suppose you think I'm mad, talking about magic.'

'No', said Cuffee. 'There is a magic in all things. Life is a sort of magic. If it was by magic you came, then you may return by the same magic. You have to learn how to use the magic.'

Mattie was surprised by Cuffee's words. He made magic sound as commonplace as an electric light. Mind you, an electric light *would* be magic in this world, wouldn't it?

Just then, Mattie's watch played *Yankee Doodle*.

He stared at it in disbelief. 'I ask you,' he thought, 'it stays broken all day, then it does this to me!'

Mattie looked around the room. The people in the cottage didn't jump in surprise, or fall on their knees. They didn't do any of the other things people from the past are supposed to do when they encounter the marvels of the modern age. No, they *laughed*! Only the big man in the corner remained aloof and apart.

Mattie shrugged his shoulders: 'Magic.'

'Magic,' grinned Kota.

The laughter put Mattie at ease. He returned to his question: 'What year is this?'

Cuffee frowned. 'The white man talks of years. We only talk of days since we came here. There is sleep tonight and there is work tomorrow. On Sunday there is rest. That is all.'

'But you must count the years!' said Mattie.

'We did once, but that was in Africa,' said the woman. 'Here, the white man says: "My way is the only way." Our ways are crushed and broken.'

Mattie gave up. If they did know the year, they weren't saying.

The big man continued to stare into the darkness. There was a deep, brooding silence about him. His face was like a mask. Mattie wondered what had happened to him to strike him dumb. Was he a victim of torture, a witness of sights too terrible to bear, or was it just a natural affliction?

Kota noticed Mattie looking at the big man. 'That

is Brother No-one.' he said. 'This is Cuffee's wife, Adjaba. This is Affrul, and that is baby Kola.'

Mattie looked at their faces. Cuffee's features were soft; both friendly and sad. Adjaba, in contrast looked fierce and proud.

But it was the mask-like face of Brother No-one which stayed with him as he fell into a fitful sleep.

# CHAPTER FIVE

# Masks

Mattie lay in that dream-like state somewhere between sleeping and waking. As he slipped again into an uneasy dream, he was aware of himself looking up through running water at a face, a mask-like face hovering above him. The face also seemed to be made of water. It trembled and changed like water whose surface ripples in a strong breeze. It trembled and changed. It formed and re-formed and each time a new face hovered above him.

Brother No-one's expressionless face looked as if it was made of carved and polished wood. The eyes were like fires burning intensely in the darkness. The water shook. Kota smiled through the shivering, changing current. 'Watch they don't cut your throat,' he said. The water shook again, and this time Pravin murmured: 'Do you want me to go, Mattie? Do you want me to go?'

Sunlight blazed on the water. It was hard and cruel and brilliant – not a life-giving light. It was the taker of life. Burns tapped on the water with his whip. He said: 'Who ran, Mattie? Who ran? You know the price for running.' He raised his whip and brought it down. The sunlight burst into a storm of cascading droplets on the surface. It settled again and reformed. Tony Doran was staring down. A mocking smile played on his lips.

'Whose side are you on, Mattie? Whose side are you on?'

Suddenly, Mattie was running from the faces, running from their taunts and demands. He ran, but he could not escape. He was treading water. The faces revolved around him, demanding: 'Whose side are you on?'

Mattie sat upright. He was panting and crying. Cuffee gently shook his shoulder.

'Wake up, Mattie. It was a dream, just a dream. You have dreamed of your fear. Now, you must find the hope to drive out the fear.'

Cuffee handed something to him. Mattie stared at the bowl.

'It's food. Rice and yam. Eat it, and you'll feel better.'

Mattie took another look. He wasn't at all sure he *would* feel better – he was an egg and chips sort of boy. It was better than nothing, though, so he ate.

The first rays of dawn stretched across the earth floor of the cottage. He heard the cock crowing and slaves moving about outside, tending their plots. They must have been working since before dawn. Adjaba was sitting in the doorway, nursing her baby with one arm, and pounding something in an earthenware pot with the other. Kota appeared, his bare feet slapping the brown earth. He greeted Mattie with a broad grin and Mattie returned the smile. As Cuffee left the cottage, Mattie said:

'I like your father. He's kind.'

'Father? You must mean Cuffee. He isn't my father. He's the Obeah-man.'

Mattie looked puzzled.

'Don't you know what that means? Obeah-man means magic man. He took me in after my mother died. My real father was sold to another plantation in the Blue Mountains.'

Mattie thought of his own mother. She must be worried sick.

Suddenly, a question came into his mind. 'Kota, why did you call me the Irishman? Cuffee said it too.'

Kota shrugged his shoulders. 'You'll have to ask him. He told me that you were the Irishman's boy. I don't even know what an Irishman is, do you?'

'Yes,' said Mattie, 'an Irishman is –'

He didn't finish. The sound of raised voices came from outside.

'Get out of here, Elisha. Get back to the white man's house, or we'll bury you and leave you to the ants.'

It was Cuffee's voice, full of anger.

Another voice replied, wheedling and sly: 'You are the one who will be buried, Obeah-man. I know you are planning something. When I find out what it is, you are a dead man.'

Kota whispered: 'That is Elisha. He is a creole.'

'What's that?'

'It means he was born here, not in Africa. He takes the white man's part. All the other house-slaves are terrified of him. He only has to point his finger at someone and Burns will flog them. Elisha hates Cuffee. He would do anything to have him killed. That's why –'

Kota stopped short. 'Soon you will understand. I can

51

say no more.'

The shell-bugle sounded.

Kota said: 'I have to go. Burns is calling us to the fields. Stay here. We will try to find a way to get you off the plantation tonight. Whatever you do, don't leave the cottage. There is salt-fish and rice in that pot, and fresh water in the other one.'

Kota touched Mattie briefly on the shoulder then scurried off to join the slaves as they set out for the fields. Mattie waited until silence settled over the village. He stole a glance outside. The slaves were already out of sight, at work in the fields. In the opposite direction stood the big house. It looked grander than ever in the daylight.

But the house only held Mattie's attention for a second. He had seen something else. In the square, around which the slave quarters were arranged, sat a man. He was bound to a tree trunk so tightly that he could barely move.

What drew Mattie's eyes to the slave wasn't the way he was bound, but his face. It was completely covered by an iron mask, held in place by two iron bands. One ran around the back of the slave's head, the other ran over the top of his skull and was padlocked to the first.

Of the slave's features, only his eyes were visible. Mattie gasped audibly. He was fascinated and appalled at the same time. He watched as the slave shifted his weight to relieve the discomfort of the mask. Sometimes he would raise his head, sometimes he would rest his chin on his breast. He was unable to ease the pressure of the mask.

The sun rose in the sky. Hours passed. Mattie tried to occupy himself. He looked round the cottage, but there was little to see. The slaves had few belongings; some pots of herbs and powders, some utensils, a little clothing. On the wall hung two carved ritual masks. Their faces were quite expressionless. Repeatedly, Mattie was drawn back to the doorway where he could see the slave twisting and shifting. Then, when the sun was bright in the sky, he began to moan and cry out. Mattie tried to shut out the man's cries, but he couldn't. He scanned the estate, it seemed deserted. He remembered Kota's warning: 'Whatever you do, don't leave the cottage.'

Mattie rested his head against the wooden wall of the cottage. He closed his eyes, but one image filled his mind: the iron mask. He picked up the food and water. He was shaking. His legs felt weak. He looked left and right. To his left, he could see the track which led away to the cane fields. To his right, he could now make out the smoke and steam of the sugar factory. Here and there, a figure was moving, but only in the distance and oblivious of the village square. Mattie pressed himself against the doorway of the cottage.

He had never imagined that taking a single step could be such an undertaking. He trembled, he hesitated, then at last he crept into the sunlight. He darted a furtive look first towards the fields, then back towards the refining sheds. Nobody had seen him.

It seemed to take an age but at last he reached the slave's side.

'Don't say anything,' he hissed, 'I'm a friend. I've brought you some water.'

The slave started. He began to turn his head. Mattie shrank back and said: 'No, look ahead, or we will both be in danger.'

Mattie again checked the plantation. Smoke and steam were drifting into a clear, blue sky. Not a soul stirred. Mattie lifted the jug so the slave could drink. It was impossible. Food was also out of the question. The full horror of the mask struck Mattie. While the slave wore it, he could neither eat nor drink.

Mattie thought quickly. He pulled out his handkerchief. It was spotted with blood from his fall at Heywood House, but this was no time to worry about hygiene. Mattie soaked the handkerchief in the water and eased it under the mask. The slave was able to suck a little water from it.

Mattie repeated the operation until the slave said: 'Thank you, friend. Let me see your face.'

Mattie backed away. 'No, you must not.'

The slave was quiet for a moment, then he said:

'If I am not to know who you are, let me at least tell you my name. I am Yambo. I am a warrior, the son of warriors. My crime is that I told Burns to call me by my real name. He mocks me with the name Nero. I have worn this mask for days. Friends bring me water under the cover of darkness, but they can't come in the daylight hours. That is when they are at work in the fields. You have given me the strength to endure until nightfall.'

'You have given me strength too, Yambo. Listen, I must go. Don't let them break you.'

Mattie made for the cottage. When he was just two strides from the door, he came face to face with a little white boy.

The boy was no more than three or four. Mattie froze, then realized that a parent or nurse couldn't be far behind. He turned and ran around the corner of the hut, and out of the boy's sight. The boy was yelling at the top of his voice: 'A boy! I saw a white boy. Come quickly!'

Mattie caught sight of a cluster of cottonwood trees

between the slave quarters and the sugar factory. He made straight for it. As he flung himself to the ground behind the trees, he saw the boy come running into sight, followed by a woman.

'Come quickly, come quickly. I saw him. You've got to tell the men.'

# CHAPTER SIX

# Heywood of Liverpool

The child continued to insist that he had seen a strange white boy. He evaded every attempt by the woman to grab his wrist. At last she began to lose her patience.

'You come here, master William. Come away from this dreadful place. If we don't leave this moment, we might encounter one of those vile heathens. Oh, do come along.'

'I'll find him, Margaret. I won't go till I find him.'

The woman finally succeeded in trapping the boy, and he began to wail at the top of his voice. She was clearly a maidservant, but she looked rich in comparison to the slaves.

Mattie watched with relief as the woman dragged master William by the hand towards the sugar factory.

He was shouting: 'I'll tell on you Margaret. You're

not supposed to see that man Henry. If you don't let me go, I'll tell, just you see.'

'And if you tell, I shan't let you have jam on your bread, just *you* see.'

At that master William conceded defeat.

Mattie lay low as the pair hurried by, still bickering. Margaret finally reached the workshops by means of a few threats and not a little bribery. While a disappointed master William continued to look around for his strange white boy, Margaret stood a little apart from the slaves who were working in the sheds. Her determination to see 'that man' overcame her evident disgust for them.

From his hiding-place Mattie could see into the sugar factory. Slaves were at work stoking a great furnace, tossing bundles of sugar canes into a roller, or ladling the extracted juice into great vats. Their skins were blasted by the tremendous heat.

Suddenly Margaret's expression brightened. She waved to an overseer who was striding across the floor of a shed which stored the cane. She was smiling broadly. He returned her smile. The child was squirming to be free of Margaret's grasp. He wanted to find that white boy.

A scream shattered the busy routine of the workshops. A woman rolled on the ground, tearing at a hot, sticky paste which was clinging to her arm. She had been splashed by the liquid sugar, which she had been stirring. Two men ran to her aid, pouring cold water over the scalded limb. Their action infuriated the overseer. He guided Margaret and master William into a tiny, ramshackle office, then marched across the boiling-house to the scene of the accident. He seized one of the helpers by the shoulder and roughly pushed him away from the moaning woman.

'Why have you stopped working? Do you think it takes two of you to help one clumsy slave? And why are the rest of you gawping? Just think yourselves lucky it wasn't you. You, Quashie, take her back to her cottage, and make sure you hurry back. I'm losing production. Now, all of you, back to work!'

Hostile eyes stared at the overseer in silent contempt. No one moved. Mattie leaned forward despite himself. It was the second time he had detected defiance among the slaves.

The overseer was struggling to gain control over the labourers. 'I said back to work, damn you!'

A note of anxiety entered his voice. 'Come on, you black wretches! No work, no food.'

In desperation, he seized a teenage girl by the wrist.

'Do you want to see her on the whipping tree? I can set to work this very moment if that's what you wish.'

The slaves looked on. A dozen pairs of eyes turned first to the scalded woman, then to the overseer and his sobbing hostage. The overseer began pushing people, and lashing at them with his whip. Even then, they barely gave ground. Their anger was building up like a wall – each glare, each grimace was one more brick. Mattie felt as if there was a power running through the air and the earth. He could almost touch it. He could feel its force.

'You, get into that shed. You too. Run! All of you. To work!'

At last the overseer took control. The slaves dropped their heads one by one. They shuffled their feet. A moment before, they had been united. Now, they stood apart from one another, each feeling his or her own fear. The overseer wiped the sweat from his eyes. He was in command again. He relaxed his grip on the girl's wrist.

'That's it, enough of this nonsense. Quashie, get that woman to her cottage. The rest of you, work!' There was obvious relief in his voice as he issued his orders.

As work resumed, Margaret and master William emerged from the office. The moment they stepped into the shed, master William screamed: 'He's there. He's there. Look! Look!'

Mattie realized his mistake in creeping forward during the confrontation. As he tried to squirm back behind the trees, he heard Henry say:

'Margaret, if you don't shut him up, I shan't answer for the consequences!'

'Now then, master William,' said Margaret. 'Enough of this nonsense. Is there somewhere we can go, Henry, away from this terrible place?'

'Aye, but just for a moment. They need constant supervision, these slaves.'

If Margaret and Henry didn't believe the boy, somebody did. A slave turned at master William's words and looked straight at Mattie's hiding-place. He made sure that Henry, Margaret and the child had left the workshop, then gestured to Mattie. He held up a canvas sheet. Mattie crawled underneath. Just then, he heard the voices returning.

'How do you put up with this job, Henry? Not one of them wants to put in a hard day's work. They're idlers, every one of them, and insolent, to cap it all.'

Their footsteps came within a hair's breadth of the tarpaulin. Mattie heard Margaret protesting: 'What are you doing? Why are you trying to shut me up?'

'I would speak more quietly, if I were you, Margaret. I fear that the slightest provocation might start a riot. We can't have these little trysts of ours starting a slave revolt now, can we?'

Margaret lowered her voice. 'Watch what you say in front of master William.' She paused for a moment. 'Surely you don't believe there could be a riot?'

The overseer's voice was lost in a roar from the furnace, then Mattie heard him say: 'There are enough of the black devils who have taken to the hills these past few years. Even the troops are reluctant to go into the forest after them. They say it's like chasing a shadow, pursuing these slave bands. Do you remember the old carpenter? He's one that joined them. He took one of our best muskets with him. It has been worse than ever these last few months. I'm afraid that something is brewing.'

Mattie discovered an eyelet in the canvas sheet. He glimpsed the look of fear on Margaret's face. She hugged the child tightly as if one of the sugar workers might spring from the mill and carry him off to the hills.

'Riot indeed!' she snorted.

Master William took advantage of the pause in the conversation and wailed: 'But what about the boy?'

'Oh come on then,' said Henry. 'Let's have a look for this boy of yours.'

For a couple of minutes Mattie could only hear the sounds of the sugar process, then he caught Henry's voice again. '*Now* will you stop chattering about white boys hiding everywhere?'

'But he was there,' protested master William. 'He *was*.'

Mattie peered through the eyelet, to see Margaret hurrying off in the direction of the big house. The overseer grinned. He enjoyed giving her a fright. Then he looked at the slaves, and an expression of concern spread over his face.

Mattie settled in for a long wait under the tarpaulin.

He still had the salt-fish and rice tucked in his jacket. He chewed the fish hungrily and cast his mind back to Henry's words. Slave revolt. Was it possible? Before he could come to any firm conclusion, the corner of the tarpaulin twitched, and the slave who had spotted him slid nimbly in next to him.

'You must be the Irishman's boy.'

Mattie didn't bother denying it. He nodded to make things easier.

It did the trick.

'Adjaba told me that there was a stranger in her cottage. Only the Obeah-man could befriend a white boy.'

Mattie cut the man's conversation short. 'Will I be safe here?'

'Safe? Of course you'll be safe. I know every man and woman in these sheds. We're bound together like a bundle of canes. The knife can't cut you when you are all as one. Isn't that true?'

Mattie wasn't sure if he was meant to say yes. It didn't matter. The man ran on as though possessed.

'What are you doing here? You should be in the Obeah-man's cottage.'

Mattie whispered an explanation of the suffering of the slave in the iron mask. The man was listening intently. Sometimes he frowned, sometimes he smiled. Mattie took in the details of his face. On his forehead he bore the pale, scarred outlines of the letters 'SH'. His right ear had been half-severed. The man saw Mattie staring. He took the boy's fingers and pressed them to the marks on his face.

'What do you think of my brand marks, Irish? Burns put them on me with the hot iron.'

The slave lifted his shapeless white vest. 'Look here. This was because I tried to run. It took them a whole afternoon to catch me. They cropped my ear for me too.'

Mattie couldn't conceal his feelings of disgust. The man enjoyed the effect of his story for a moment, then peered through the eyelet in the tarpaulin.

'I thought I heard someone coming. I thought it might be Elisha. He is a wicked man, that Elisha. Look out for him, Irish. The white man gave him some cast-off silks and a job as the head house-servant. He struts around the place and thinks he is very grand. He is not to be trusted. He is Burns' eyes and ears. If he finds you, you will be one dead white boy.'

The slave grinned. 'Stay there boy. I will get a message to Cuffee.'

The man winked then flicked at his mutilated ear with his forefinger. It was an odd gesture. Mattie winced.

Once again, the man enjoyed the effect it had on Mattie, then he raised the tarpaulin, poked out his head, and sprang into the open. Mattie's mind filled with all sorts of terrors. Why did adults have to do that, scare you that way? Even uncle Johnny, good and kindhearted as he was, loved to tease.

Mattie made himself comfortable, or at least a bit less uncomfortable. He rested his head against a barrel. It was marked: SAMUEL HEYWOOD OF LIVERPOOL. Mattie peered inside at a dark, sticky substance. He put in his finger and tasted it. Treacle, or something very like it. He grimaced. He hated treacle.

On the ground by the barrel lay a few copies of a yellowed and crumpled newspaper, *The Jamaica Gazette*. Mattie leafed through them. He discovered stories which made his blood run cold.

In a column headed 'Runaway Slaves' he read:

'Caesar, marked on the right shoulder, TM. Heart and arrow between, and on the left TM and arrow.' Then:

'Scipio, a cooper, branded on both cheeks and on the breast WM. A runaway.'

He read about a woman slave who had attacked an overseer with a shovel. She was 'still abroad'.

He thought of the man with whom he had just been speaking. He thought of the branding iron on his flesh, the mutilated ear. It must be commonplace. He read on:

'An old grey-headed Coromantee man. Marked on both shoulders SH. Branded on the back with a cattle mark. Whoever shall apprehend the said man, alive or dead, shall receive a generous reward from RALPH HOWARD BURNS.'

Mattie looked again at the words on the barrel. Samuel Heywood of Liverpool: SH. He breathed deeply and rested his head on the barrel. So this is how you built your fine house, Samuel Heywood! This is how.

While Samuel Heywood filled his house with treasures, his ships were crossing and re-crossing the Atlantic. They carried manufactured goods, trinkets and guns to Africa. In exchange they bought human souls and transported them here to Jamaica to work the cane fields. From Jamaica, the Heywood ships returned to England loaded with sugar – the stuff fortunes were made of.

His mind spinning, Mattie leafed randomly through the newspaper until he discovered another item:

'Slave Disturbance.' It read: 'In St Anne's parish a disturbance has recently been suppressed. Involving some eighty slaves of the Coromantin nation, the outbreak affected two plantations. Ringleaders have been hanged.'

It was this mountain of injustice that supported all the riches of Heywood House. Every brick a slave, every trowel of mortar a branding; each tile, each lick of paint a human life.

# CHAPTER SEVEN

# The Irishman

It was quiet now in the sugar factory. The furnaces had been banked down for the night. Mattie heard footsteps coming closer. He peered through the eyelet. It was quite dark, so he had to rely upon his hearing. The footsteps slapped on the ground. They were made by bare feet so it was almost certain that they belonged to a friend. Bare feet meant slaves. Sure enough, Kota's head popped under the canvas.

'You dance close to the fire, Mattie. Watch you don't get burned.'

Mattie smiled sheepishly. He had expected the sternest telling-off for disobeying the order not to leave the cottage. Instead, he could detect a note of admiration in Kota's teasing.

'Follow me. Keep that white head of yours low. Elisha

has been sniffing around.'

Mattie held back.

'What's wrong?' asked Kota.

'A little boy saw me. What if somebody believed him?'

'Nobody is going to believe him. Do you think many whites would go roaming around the slave quarters unless they had to be there? The woman, Margaret, only comes down here to see her man, and the people at the big house don't know about it. Besides, Cuffee has posted look-outs around the cottages.'

Mattie still hesitated. 'Shouldn't you keep things quiet until I have gone? Let me find my own way out of here. It is dangerous for you all to take risks for me.'

Kota looked as if he would laugh out loud. 'Being here is the great danger, Mattie.'

Mattie reluctantly followed Kota. The two boys stooped low and raced across the open ground between the workshops and the village. The closer they came to the village, the more the air filled with the sounds of music and singing.

Mattie gave Kota a questioning look. Kota drew his friend into the safety of the cottage. 'Do you like it? It's a celebration for Yambo. His punishment ended today. The overseers won't come near. It's Sunday tomorrow. No work.'

Mattie couldn't quite get used to the idea that anyone might live like this and yet still enjoy a festival. Still, he told himself, remember the golden rule. Don't worry about it. Just get on with it.

'I love the celebrations,' said Kota. 'We call them Junkanoos.'

Eight or ten drummers were beating out a fast, surging rhythm. They had all kinds of drums; congas and tom-toms, tall drums and hand drums, drums you played by hand and drums you played with beaters. Then there were men playing gourds strung with animal hair. Others played shakers of every description. A flute or two made up the array of instruments. There were dancers wearing ritual masks. The glow of the village fires was reflected in the faces of performers and spectators, but maybe a little of the glow came from inside them. They were chanting: 'Alla! Alla!'

At the end of a broad path, the big house was dimly lit by oil lamps. Between the slave quarters and the great, white building lay so much more than physical distance.

Kota put his hand on Mattie's. 'Cuffee wants to see you.'

Mattie had been smiling at the sights and sounds of the Junkanoo. The smile vanished from his face at Kota's words. 'This is where I get told off,' he thought.

Kota and Mattie found Cuffee sitting in the doorway of the cottage closest to the cane fields. It was darker there. The glow of the fires barely lit the faces of the people around the doorway. Adjaba was nursing her sleeping baby, and stroking Affrul's dark, curly hair. Brother No-one sat as still and silent as ever, his eyes trained on the darkness beyond the village.

There were two older men in the cottage. They were the only old people Mattie had seen. One stared steadily into Mattie's face. The other, as tall and thin as any man Mattie had ever seen or imagined, sat cross-legged. His beard was almost completely white. When at last he raised his face, Mattie could see that he was blind. Cuffee patted the earth beside him. Mattie sat down and looked from Cuffee to Adjaba. He wanted some word or gesture which might tell him if he was in trouble. Adjaba ignored him, but Cuffee's eyes were warm and friendly.

It was the blind man who spoke:

'The Obeah-man tells me that you are not the Irish-man's boy.'

Mattie's reply tumbled out in a rush:

'No, I'm not. I've never heard of your Irishman. Whoever he is, I don't know anything about him. I'm no spy though. I didn't know about you, or Burns, Heywood, or anything until I came here . . .'

Should he have mentioned Heywood? He had heard of Heywood before, in that great, mysterious house on the other side of the painting. He hadn't known then what it was that lay behind the wealth of the house, despite the evidence which hung on the walls.

Mattie had another attempt at explaining, but the blind man spoke over his voice:

'I can see you know nothing of the Irishman. I hoped you knew him, you see. I wanted to meet him just once more before I died. I was a boy when the sailors brought me across the seas. I was no older than you. I cried for my mother and my father all night long. I lay upon the earth when they took me out into the fields to work. I would neither lift a knife to cut cane, nor would I talk. The overseer tied me to a cart, and drew his whip. The Irishman took the whip from him and cut me free. From then on I learned to keep my head low and work, until the day came that I might again walk as a free man among my own people. I still wait for that day.'

'Who was the Irishman?' asked Mattie.

'In the days before I came to this country, when they were setting up the first plantations, poor white men worked the cane. They sold themselves as bondsmen. When they had worked out their time, they were free men again. The Irishman worked the fields for seven years to earn his freedom. He was already a free man, that day he saved me from the lash. He was a blacksmith. He was the first white man I ever knew who dared to help a slave, or cared to. The first, and the last, until you.'

Mattie couldn't believe his ears. He had heard about slavery, but never about white slaves!

'What happened to the bondsmen?' he asked.

'I can't say for certain. I think they were too few and sold themselves only for a brief time, perhaps five or ten years. This land devours men and women. We Africans are many and our labour is for life. The Irishman was the only bondsman I ever saw. I did want to meet him again. I wanted to know *why*, that's all. Why did he risk himself to help me?'

'You never heard of him after that?' Mattie asked.

The blind man shook his head. 'Only rumours. I heard he was ruined by the plantation owners. They say he went to the Americas to start a new life. I hope he lived a long and happy one.'

Mattie paused for a second. 'Is that it? Are there no more white people who have spoken out against this?'

It was Cuffee who replied. He spoke bitterly: 'Why should they? Stand the house of the planter next to the house of the slave. There you have your answer. Even Burns stands far above us, drunken, stupid fool though he is. He has money for grog. He has his own room, filled with his own belongings. Do you know he boasts to us about this? Most of all, he knows that one day he will return to his own land.'

'But there will be people who will speak out against slavery. One day it will end.'

The others laughed or shook their heads at Mattie's outburst.

'Who will end it?' Cuffee said. 'The planters call the

sugar white gold. It is life to them.'

'And death to us.'

The voice belonged to Adjaba. She was the last to speak for some time. The group turned their faces towards the musicians and singers. Then the blind man said: 'Kota, it is time to run your message.'

Kota set off, weaving between the drummers and the singers.

Mattie was too bound up with his own thoughts to notice him return in the company of Yambo.

'I have brought someone to meet you, Mattie,' said Kota.

Mattie looked up. He didn't recognize Yambo as the man in the mask.

'Do I look different without the mask? I had to thank you. I couldn't believe it when they told me.'

Mattie passed a hand over his face. He didn't know what to say.

Yambo continued: 'You should have seen the look on Burns' face. Each day he came to look at me, thinking I would be begging for mercy. He didn't know that I had friends who would risk their lives to bring me water. Now he thinks I can live without food and water. That scares him half to death.'

Yambo roared with laughter at the thought of Burns' disappointment. His eyes were gleaming.

'Burns will wish he had killed me instead of putting me in the mask. Isn't that right, Cuffee? Soon, we will wipe the smile from his face. We'll do it soon, isn't that right, Obeah-man?'

Adjaba stood up and snapped: 'Enough, you fool! Your tongue will be the death of us.'

It wasn't the first time Adjaba had stopped the men talking in Mattie's presence. She glared at Yambo.

'Get back to the Junkanoo. Put that mouth of yours to its proper use. Join the singers.'

Yambo waved gaily and returned to the Junkanoo. Adjaba confided in her husband: 'Yambo has a strong arm, but he talks too much. Don't take him into your confidence.'

Cuffee nodded.

'You've made a friend in Yambo,' said Kota, squatting next to Mattie. Mattie didn't reply. He was thinking of another friend.

'What's wrong, Mattie? I thought you'd be happy. Cuffee thinks you were very brave.'

'Today, maybe,' said Mattie. 'But I let down a friend in my own time.' Kota stared at Mattie. 'Your time? You've said that before. What do you mean?'

'I came here from the future. At least, I think that's it. I am from the times to come'.

The blind man started at Mattie's words. 'The times to come! Is the boy right in the head?'

'Mattie is not of this place,' Cuffee said. 'We all know that. He doesn't speak like us, or like Burns. We felt from the first that he was different. There are so many things we don't understand. I don't doubt what he says.'

'Do they have slaves in your time?' Kota asked.

Mattie shook his head.

'Then is it a paradise?' asked the second old man.

'No, it isn't a paradise. How can I explain it to you? People are still cruel. We even have people like Burns, but we don't have slaves. They abolished slavery years ago, before I was born.'

'I am glad,' said Cuffee. 'If there is a time when there are no slaves, only free men, then life is worth living. It is my dream, that my children will live as free people.'

Mattie wanted to tell them that everything was going

to be all right, that a new day was dawning in which slavery would be gone forever. He wanted to tell them that there was a better time and a better place. In many ways there was, but if people said 'no' to the likes of Tony Doran and the people who filled his head with hatred, the world might be even better. Suddenly things looked clearer to him. 'If only I could go back somehow,' he thought. 'If only I could put things right.'

He listened to the singers and sank into his own memories and thoughts. Nobody interrupted his brooding. The fires were burning low when he raised his head from his arms. The drums had fallen silent and a single voice soared over the village. The song was haunting and sad. Mattie's ability to decipher the language of the slaves deserted him. The words of the song would not yield their mystery.

'What's the song about, Kota?' he asked.

'That's Yambo singing. He is singing about the living, about his ancestors who he will join at the hour of his death, and about those who are waiting to be born.'

Yambo ended his song. There followed another singer. This man's voice was deeper. Though his song was no less sad, it sounded fierce and proud. Mattie searched among the field slaves for the singer. Kota pointed. It was Brother No-one, standing alone in the shadows.

'But I thought . . .'

'That he couldn't speak? He chooses not to speak. I will ask him to explain, if you want me to.'

'Please.'

When Brother No-one ended his song, he came over and sat down with Kota and Mattie.

This is the story he told.

# CHAPTER EIGHT

## Brother No-one's Story

'I was a master craftsman in my own village. They said I could make things of wood talk. I had a wife who was beautiful and wise. She bore me two children.

'One day I was ordered to go to the court of the King, at his palace at the mouth of the river. I was to carve a shrine to the gods. On my arrival I found that there was a great ship there, a slaver. The King agreed to trade slaves for pistols, gunpowder, cutlasses, knives and other goods brought from across the seas.

'I watched as he bargained with the ship's captain. His name was Gordon. Captain Gordon said: "These are for you, great King and slave-maker. In trade I want 100 slaves, men and women. I want no children. They always die and they're more trouble than they're worth."

'The King laughed. "You shall have your slaves" he

73

said. "Give me twenty of your men and my army shall set out tomorrow. Remember to tell your own people that I am the great King, the buyer of pistols and gunpowder, the seller of men and women."

'I felt a tightness in my chest. Imagine my despair when I overheard a soldier speaking. One of the villages to be raided was my own. I set out that night to reach my village. I arrived before dawn and woke the people. They fled into the forest, but there was to be no escape. The King and Captain Gordon had many men, armed with muskets and cutlasses. We were hunted down and taken away, yoked together. Some of the children were left behind with those of our people who were too old to be of use to Gordon. We begged to take our children with us. We could not bear to be parted from them. My wife and I looked such strong workers that we were allowed to keep our children. If only we had known what the journey was to be like.

'I had to watch as my wife and children were branded. The slave-traders must have seen my hatred for them – they branded me on my chest, then on my back. When they heard that I was a carpenter, they branded me on the palms of my hands. They stood laughing as I choked back my cries.

'The branding was nothing compared to the sea passage. It was a terrible voyage. We were chained and packed together so that we could barely move. There was no air, and the heat was terrible. I was chained apart from my family. I could barely understand my neighbour. He was an Ashanti, captured by Gordon some weeks before. That is how they kept control of so many, you see, by keeping us apart from our own people. The divided us, sitting Ibo next to Coromantee, Coromantee next to Ashanti, Ashanti next to Yoruba.

I had to look on helplessly as my children weakened.

'At dawn each morning we were brought up onto the deck to exercise to the beat of the drum. Captain Gordon yelled: "Jump, you black devils, jump!" He carried a whip to force us to do as he said. I heard a sailor shout: "See them jump for joy!"

'One day my boys were dead. We did not see them being put into the sea. The crew just carried them away with the rest of the dead. They say the waters were full of sharks following the ship, feeding on our people. Two days later, my wife followed her sons.

'When they set me to work in this place, I was already a dead man walking. All my dreams lie out in that ocean. I listen for their voices on every sea breeze.

'Now, Mattie, I will tell you how I came by my name. Burns gave me my tools for work in the fields. I let them fall from my hand. I wanted to join my wife and boys in the land of the dead. I thought that this would be the quickest way. Burns screamed at me. I said: "I am a free man. I am a craftsman. I will not work for you."

'Elisha explained my words to Burns. He was a common field-slave then, but would do anything to get a job in the master's house. Burns laughed at me: "You are nothing. You are what I want you to be. Do you hear me? You are no one." I was flogged until I was senseless. The next day, I was flogged again. I would not work. Burns was trembling with anger.

'On the fourth day Burns woke me. I saw a woman tied to a whipping post. It was Adjaba. It was Elisha's idea. That is how he became a house-slave, by helping Burns crush us. I could not allow Adjaba to suffer for my pride. I agreed to work. Since that day, she and Cuffee have been my greatest friends. Everyone calls me Brother No-one. What was an insult in the mouth of Burns, is the only thing that makes me a man.'

After Brother No-one had finished speaking, everyone
sat silently for a long time, until the slave with half an
ear came running and whispered something in Cuffee's
ear.

Cuffee walked over to Mattie. 'We had planned to
help you escape tonight, under the cover of darkness.
We were only waiting for the lights to go out in the
big house. But I've just been told that there are soldiers
camping in the hills – they're pursuing escaped slaves.
Now you'll have to remain here until they've left the
district.'

# CHAPTER NINE

# Slave Sunday

Mattie slept on until well after dawn. There was no conch-shell call to work on this Sunday morning, but he woke to a buzz of activity in the village outside. The slaves were working on the plots of land which provided them with yams, potatoes and plantains. Mattie reached for his clothes only to find a white, threadbare shirt and frayed, shapeless trousers. He felt around on the floor of the cottage. His clothes had gone!

Kota walked in. 'It's about time you woke up,' he said. 'Is this the way life is in the times to come? Lying in bed until the middle of the morning?

Mattie ignored him. 'Where are my clothes?' he demanded. 'They were right here last night.'

Kota pinched his nose between thumb and forefinger. 'They smelt, so Adjaba washed them in the river. She

77

gave them a good pounding on the stones. She is trying to find somewhere to dry them where the overseers won't see them.'

Mattie leapt out of the two thin sheets which served as a bed. 'Washed them! Oh, not my jacket. It says 'dry clean only' on the label. It will look a mess.'

Kota couldn't make head nor tail of 'dry cleaning.' 'I doubt if rolling it about in the dust would make it clean. It stank of salt-fish.'

Mattie suddenly remembered where he was, and what his friends had to put up with. He felt ashamed. All that fuss about a jacket! It *was* a Boss jacket though.

He glanced at his watch. One thirty. It was still one thirty. The man in the shop said it was shock-proof, water-proof and boy-proof. It would take a B-52 bomber to damage this little miracle of technology, he had told Mattie. 'Tell it to the marines,' thought Mattie.

He dressed in the clothes Adjaba had left out for him. They were like hospital pyjamas. Mattie felt self-conscious, but Kota paid no attention. Resigned to looking like a long-stay case from the hospital, Mattie ate the breakfast Kota had handed him. It still wasn't egg and chips, but it took away the hollow feeling in his stomach.

The moment Mattie pushed away the empty bowl, Kota tossed over a broad-brimmed hat, and said: 'Put that on. We're going out.' Mattie jerked to attention. 'I can't. I'd stick out like a sore thumb.'

'Thumb? What are you talking about? Now, put on that hat. Pull the brim low over your eyes and keep your hands inside your sleeves. Ready? Come on. Cuffee's waiting.'

The boys found Cuffee waiting for them at the edge of the village. He greeted Mattie with a smile. 'Well, Mattie, do you remember how you came here with Kota?

You will have to retrace your steps in the dark tonight if you want to find your way home.'

'I think I know the way,' said Mattie. 'Of course, I was thinking more about the men who were chasing us at the time. I find it hard to think when I've got a gun at my back.'

Mattie winced at his own words. Oh, this is a great time to go quoting John Wayne!

Cuffee took no notice. He laid out every stage in the journey. As he spoke, he pointed out landmarks in the distance. He was able to explain the route as far as the hillside but knew the way no further. Kota told Mattie what he recalled. It was up to Mattie to do the rest.

As they discussed the route he would have to follow, a thought dawned on Mattie.

'Cuffee, did you send Kota up to the hillside for some reason. Is that why he was there?'

Cuffee stared at Mattie. His eyes were suddenly cold. Mattie had entered forbidden territory. He quickly said: 'I didn't mean to pry. I . . .'

Cuffee dismissed him with a frown. 'Do you think you will be all right on your own?'

'Yes,' said Mattie, wondering why what he said had so disturbed Cuffee. He tried to sound confident. He wasn't. In his heart he was deeply afraid. What if Burns was out there, or Elisha? What if he encountered the soldiers?

Kota gave him a dig in the ribs with his elbow. 'Wake up you dreamer. You'll make it. I did and I don't know any magic.'

Mattie looked at Kota. 'If Joanne was here, that's the sort of thing she would say,' he thought.

Mattie returned Kota's dig in the ribs, setting off a bout of play-wrestling. The two friends pushed and shoved and wrestled their way back across the square. Kota threw a rotten potato at Mattie. Mattie caught it and tossed it back. Soon they were in the middle of a game. It was half rugby and half soccer. Neither boy bothered to state any rules. They instinctively understood each other's idea of the game. Mattie caught the potato in one hand and raced for the cottage. Kota set off in pursuit. The boys tumbled giggling and laughing into the cottage.

Mattie was about to resume the game, when he saw Kota's eyes flash with fear. Kota put his hand over Mattie's mouth. Mattie turned so that he was propped up on one elbow, facing the doorway. There stood Burns, the overseers, John and Henry, and the house-slave, Elisha. Burns and Henry carried muskets and John carried a whip. Elisha had two more muskets slung over his shoulder.

Mattie shrank back but the four men were not concerned with the cottages. They were watching the younger children playing in the square. Elisha whispered something to Burns. Burns nodded. 'Those two will do fine. We'll see if Ebo Jack is as vain when his daughter is in service at the big house.'

Elisha beamed. Now he would have a hold over his enemy.

Kota was horrified. 'Stay here,' he hissed at Mattie, 'I've got to find Cuffee'.

He ran as fast as his legs could carry him past the men, and out of Mattie's sight.

It was then that Adjaba reached her daughter's side. She took the situation in at a glance. She dropped to her knees and begged:

'Oh, Mr Burns. Please, no, not Affrul. She is too young. Let her have her childhood. Please, I will do the work of two people.'

'Two,' sneered Burns, 'two! You can barely do your own work with that brat forever in your arms and another one trailing around your skirts. Elisha is in need of two strong young girls to be trained as house-slaves. That's the end of the matter.'

Adjaba glared fiercely at Elisha. She understood his purpose in taking the child. She looked around wildly for help.

There was none. John seized Affrul by the arm. Henry handed his musket to Elisha, and lifted Affrul's playmate off the ground. The two girls began to wail.

Mattie let out a frantic yell: 'No!' He flung himself with all his strength at John. The men were taken aback. They didn't move for what seemed an age, as Mattie tore at the overseer's face. Their eyes were wide with surprise at the sight of a strange white boy hurling himself at them with such fury. Henry looked stunned. Master William had been telling the truth, after all. John recovered sufficiently from the shock of Mattie's appearance to lash at him with his whip, but Mattie was too close to him for it to have any effect, and it brushed his shoulder harmlessly. Affrul bit John's hand and wriggled free. She ran to her mother. Burns moved against Mattie and dragged him off the beleaguered John. Even then, the struggle wasn't over. Adjaba drew a pin from her waistband and stabbed it into Henry's leg. He screamed and let go of the second girl. Adjaba seized the opportunity and made off with the two children.

Burns raised his musket and snarled: 'Stop!' But before he could fire, he found himself face to face with Cuffee, Yambo and a few of the other men who had returned with Kota. Henry and John were overpowered by sheer force of numbers. Yambo seized Henry's musket. There was a tense silence as Burns held Mattie with one arm, still pointing the musket at Adjaba's back with his free hand.

Yambo pointed the captured musket at Burns, but did not dare fire. In the distance an alarm bell was ringing, and men were running in the direction of the village.

'Not another step, Ebo Jack, or your wife is dead. Let my men go. I said, let them go! Elisha, arm them.'

In the seconds which followed, Mattie could see the agony of indecision on Cuffee's face. Cuffee hung his head and dropped the whip he had wrested from John's grasp. Yambo followed his example and reluctantly lowered the musket. A broad smile spread across Burns' face.

'Now, you are going to pay for raising your hand against those God appointed to rule over you.'

Elisha approached Burns. 'Let me administer the punishment, Mr Burns. You won't be disappointed.'

Elisha eyed Cuffee. Hatred flowed between the two men.

'I'll think about it, Elisha,' Burns said, 'now give out those muskets.'

As Mattie strained helplessly against Burns' arm, he saw the overseer's expression change, his eyes fixed on a figure who had just stepped into view.

'Why don't you use your musket, Burns, but not on Adjaba. Shoot me. I am a dead man. What have I to lose? What can you take from me that I did not lose many years past? Do you hear me Burns? Fire! But before you do, think on this. Even if you kill me, you won't have a shot left for the rest of the men in this village.'

Burns looked desperately at Elisha, but the house-slave was paralysed with fear. Brother No-one was striding towards them, closing in rapidly with each powerful step.

Then he began to run, shouting: 'You're alone Burns.'

Brother No-one moved faster, zig-zagging to leave Burns a more difficult shot. Mattie began to twist and turn with all his strength, kicking and crying out. He could smell the fear on Burns' skin.

'You're alone Burns. Alone!' Brother No-one cried again.

Burns shifted his weight, and turned the barrel of the musket on Brother No-one. Mattie gave one last great kick.

He never knew if it was his fighting back which did it, or if it was Burns' terror of Brother No-one's approach, but the musket went off. It missed its target.

Mattie felt Burns' arms go limp. He broke free and ran to Kota's side. Brother No-one wrenched the discharged musket from Burns and clubbed the overseer to the ground. He lay motionless on the earth.

Another shot suddenly splintered the wall of a cottage. The slaves turned. Five men were entering the square, running hard. They were silhouetted against the morning sun. Yambo raised his captured musket and returned fire. A white man dropped to the ground, clinging to his right leg with both hands. The two men either side of him stopped to drag him clear.

In a second, Cuffee and the man with half an ear were upon one of the two remaining men, wrestling with him.

The last of the attackers fired a shot. Brother No-one sat heavily on the ground as if felled by some great, unseen blow.

Mattie cried out and knelt anxiously by the man who could make wood talk. He looked into the mask-like face. For the first time he saw a smile.

'My legs gave way beneath me, that's all. Do you really think that they can kill me? Tell me, Mattie. How do you kill a dead man? The fool missed me. His fear betrayed him.'

Mattie looked up. The slaves had seized the three muskets from the hapless Elisha. Their volley left John and Henry lying face down on the earth. The surviving overseers were hurrying from the scene, half-carrying, half-dragging their senseless comrades towards the big house.

Burns too had made good his escape and was hobbling after them. Elisha and the man who had fired on Brother No-one were less fortunate. They were standing resigned to their fate. Yambo coolly filled his musket with powder and shot, pressed the barrel to the overseer's temple, and without a second's thought, he fired.

As the man's body crumpled, Mattie stared in horror. He looked at Yambo and cried: 'How could you?'

Yambo was re-loading the musket. He said simply: 'Maybe killing isn't the answer, but there is no choice. Now there is one less to kill our people.'

There wasn't a flicker of regret in the slaves' faces. So far, Mattie had taken their side because slavery wronged them. He sympathised with them because they suffered. Now, they were no longer content to suffer – they were fighting back. He examined the faces of Yambo, Cuffee, and Brother No-one. They were the same people they had been before the overseer's death, the killing hadn't turned them into monsters.

Yambo forced Elisha to the ground and pressed the musket to his temple.

Mattie ran over to Cuffee. 'Stop him. Please stop him.' he begged.

But Adjaba snatched the musket from Yambo and said: 'This is my job.'

Cuffee avoided Mattie's eyes. 'If it must be done,' he said in a low voice, 'take him out of the boy's sight.'

Mattie watched helplessly as Adjaba led Elisha away. A moment later a shot rang out.

Cuffee looked down at Mattie. 'Don't condemn us, Mattie. There was nothing else we could do.' Mattie turned away. 'I know.'

Cuffee looked at the anxious faces of the slaves who were now crowding around him.

'So the time has come at last,' he said. 'It is sooner than we had planned, and we are short of arms, but we must try to escape. We have gone too far to stop now.'

Brother No-one looked at Cuffee. 'You talk as if we are beaten already. They will return soon in greater numbers and will kill anyone they find. We must act.'

Yambo grinned. He alone seemed to enjoy the turn of events. 'Shall I order the digging up of the weapons, Obeah-man?'

Cuffee nodded grimly, then he looked at Mattie.

'So you know our secret at last.'

Mattie nodded. The secret was out.

# CHAPTER TEN

# Fall . . .

Mattie felt as if he was emerging from darkness into the light of day. He had read in school about slavery. He had imagined the lives of the slaves, and could understand the suffering, but he had seen them as victims, just victims. Things were done to them. They did nothing, felt nothing, were nothing. Their fate was to wait for the abolitionists to come and end the trade in human lives. But these slaves weren't prepared to wait for anyone. Mattie knew their lives were full of suffering and pain. He had never for a moment suspected that these people, who lived in the shadow of the whipping post, could have such laughter, such songs, such dreams.

All the previous night, Mattie had watched and listened as his new friends celebrated Yambo's release. He had been amazed by the Junkanoo. But he was doubly astonished by the frenzy of activity which was now unleashed. The conflict over the children had provoked a revolt which had been long in preparation. Yambo and Cuffee were stacking the improvised weapons which were being taken out of hiding. The slaves must have been planning their rising for months.

Brother No-one was organizing the slaves into teams. His silence had been broken for good. Now he was talking quickly and with authority. He was rediscovering his pride and dignity. One team gathered up what food they could muster. Another was assembling every possible weapon to resist capture.

It was a carnival of resistance.

There were cane knives, sticks and clubs. There was Burns' whip. There were shovels and rakes, and the muskets seized from the overseers. It seemed that Adjaba and Cuffee, Yambo and Brother No-one were everywhere, hurrying this group along, issuing orders to that one, listening to the worries of another. They were highly organized.

Kota raced across the square with a group of the older children.

'Where are you going?' asked Mattie.

'We are going to gather up all the belongings we can't carry with us.'

'Why?'

'Cuffee says we must burn them. We mustn't leave anything behind which could give the bloodhounds our scent.'

Mattie watched the children as they gathered their little bundles of possessions, and piled them up in the square. They were chatting and giggling as children would do in Mattie's time on Bonfire Night or on Christmas morning. Mattie stood apart. He had begun to feel at one with this community until the killings. Now, though he couldn't find it in his heart to condemn the slaves, he was unable to join in.

As they rushed off for the next pile, Mattie noticed his own clothes deposited ready for burning. He rummaged through, and found everything, including his money and bric-a-brac tied up in his handkerchief. He stepped behind a cottage and dressed quickly, leaving the threadbare rags he had been wearing on the ground in a forlorn heap. As he returned to the square, he could see Cuffee putting a torch to the pile of clothing. 'Just in the nick of time,' thought Mattie. 'It's bad enough having my smoothie jacket hand-washed, but burned. That really would be the limit!'

The plantation workers formed up in a column. The children were in the middle, protected and hidden from sight. At the front and back walked the slaves who were armed with muskets. As they left the village, they set light to the cottages in which they had tried to preserve something of the lives they had once lived as free people. A great roar went up from the column as the mean thatch and wattle huts blazed.

Adjaba led a group to fling torches into the hated cane fields. The canes began to crackle. Some of the slaves cheered and waved gaily. Others stared back anxiously through the billowing smoke watching for any sign of their pursuers. There was none as yet.

Suddenly they saw a single horseman galloping away down the coast road. Cuffee watched. 'He is going to alert the troops. We must move quickly.'

The words were not addressed to anybody in particular. Cuffee's shoulders were bowed. He looked fearful of the consequences of the revolt. Cuffee noticed Mattie looking at him. He returned his gaze, but said nothing.

The march went on into the late afternoon. The column reached a clearing in the woods at the foot of the hillside. The only evidence of the plantation was a plume of smoke rising from the burning cane fields. Cuffee ordered a few minutes rest. Men, women and children sat among the bushes, talking quietly or taking a drink. Some simply tried to reassure friends who were unable to hide their fear. Many, including Cuffee, were unable to sit down. They paced anxiously, awaiting news of the man-hunt which would surely be launched.

Mattie recognized the path up the hillside. He was five, maybe ten minutes walk from the cave. Would he reach it, and what would be there if he did? He looked across the clearing and saw the adults were grim-faced.

Not so the children! Affrul and the younger ones were listening, entranced, to the old blind man recounting the story of Anansi the spider-man and how he tricked the crocodile. Sometimes, the children anticipated the next line and chorussed the story even before the story-teller could say the words. It must have been the hundredth telling of the story. It could have been the thousandth. The childrens' eyes would still have been as bright.

Mattie moved away from the circle, he wanted to find Kota. He spotted him listening to the discussions of the leaders of the column.

Cuffee and Yambo were involved in a heated argument. Yambo wanted to stand and fight. Cuffee said their only hope was to continue marching and reach the Maroon settlements in the mountains. The Maroons were escaped slaves who had established their own communities outside the plantations.

Brother No-one interrupted: 'If we follow Yambo's advice, we will perish here, in these woods. Do you want to risk the children? Do – '

His words were cut off by the baying of bloodhounds in the distance. The sound carried in their direction. Cuffee demanded silence. He ran across the clearing and looked towards the burning cane fields.

'They are coming this way. How did they find our trail so quickly?' He turned to the half-eared man. 'Did you lay the false trail as I told you?'

The man nodded. 'The dogs should have led them out on the road towards the Gray plantation before they realized their mistake. I don't understand.'

Cuffee caught Kota by the arm and shook him like a rag doll. 'Are you sure you burned everything? Did you burn every last thing?'

Everyone was staring at the boy. Kota's eyes filled with tears. He knew he had done his job. 'I did, Cuffee. We looked everywhere.'

Mattie's face drained of blood. In his mind's eye he saw his own discarded bundle of clothes behind the hut.

Cuffee was pacing about the clearing, trying to make sense of the turn of events. He was beside himself. Mattie could see that he was blaming himself for the failure of the plan to put the dogs off their scent.

Yambo's voice broke the silence. 'Now we fight, Obeah-man. We have no choice.'

'Be quiet, you fool,' Cuffee shouted. 'If we fight, we shall die where we stand. Is that what you want?' He picked up his baby daughter. 'Is that what you want?'

Mattie stepped between the men. 'Stop it. It isn't your fault, or Kota's, or Yambo's. It was me. I left the clothes you gave me behind a cottage. I didn't know it was important. I didn't think ...' His voice trailed off. He turned away to hide his tears.

Cuffee stared at him as if he was seeing the boy for the first time, then roughly shook off Mattie's hands.

He didn't say anything, but Mattie heard the words: 'Whose side are you on?' echoing in his head.

The baying of the hounds sounded closer. Cuffee ordered Yambo to issue the arms, and send the best fighters to the front. Mattie stood alone amid the preparations for battle. He was the cause of disaster. He didn't dare think what Burns would do with the recaptured slaves.

'Wait!' cried Mattie. He clung to Cuffee. He thought for a moment that Cuffee was going to strike him. 'Listen. Please. Listen to me for one moment.'

Cuffee turned to face Mattie. He looked like somebody irritated by the incessant buzzing of a fly. 'It's me, isn't it?' Mattie said. 'I'm the one the dogs are tracking. Let me go on alone. I know somewhere I can hide. I think I can reach it before they catch me. I'm sure of it. If I reach the cave, I'm sure I can lose the dogs.'

Cuffee said nothing. Mattie tried again: 'It will give you time. You will be able to reach the forest. It's safer there. *You* told me that.'

Cuffee hesitated.

'Please let me do this.'

Adjaba stood by her husband, and nodded. Cuffee put his hand on Mattie's shoulder. It meant yes.

Mattie looked at Kota. His friend was trembling and his face was drawn. They held each other for a moment. Mattie saw Brother No-one. There was sadness in his eyes. He was looking at the children listening to the story. He had no fear for his own life, but he was desperately afraid for the children.

Without another word Mattie took to his heels. He began to climb the hillside. He was running again. This time he was not just running for his own good. He was running for every one of the people in the clearing. The baying of the dogs seemed closer than ever. Blood hammered in Mattie's chest and head. He climbed and climbed, hauling himself up the steep slope by clutching at the bushes. His eyes scanned the undergrowth for the way through to the cave. All the trees and bushes looked so alike, now that he was among them. Behind him he could hear the dogs being urged on, and the undergrowth being trampled underfoot. To his relief, he couldn't see any sign of the slave column.

Mattie plunged through a screen of bushes. What he saw on the other side made his senses reel. A waterfall tumbled twenty or thirty metres into a gorge. The cave's entrance lay beyond. Mattie had taken the wrong path. To reach his goal, he would have to retrace his steps back down the hill and begin his climb again some hundred metres to the right.

Mattie bent back a branch and squinted through it. Two bloodhounds burst through the undergrowth, panting and howling. Their front paws lifted off the ground as they strained against their handler's leash. Among the threshing bushes Mattie could make out the first of the armed men who were following the dogs. One of them was Burns. There was a blood-stained bandage round his head. He was screaming like a madman and urging the dogs on.

Mattie backed away. His sheer terror of the dogs took over. Without thinking, he flung himself into the unknown. He had no control of his movements. His legs took him back, away from the man-hunt. Suddenly there was no earth beneath his feet. He was running on air.

With a cry, he tumbled into space.

# CHAPTER ELEVEN

# ... And Rise

Mattie crashed to earth. The fall winded him. He began to roll onto his back to ease the pain, but something made him stop. Stretching out a hand behind him, Mattie felt for the ground. It wasn't there, just space.

Slowly, without daring to move his body, Mattie turned his head. The bottom of the gorge lay far below. His fall had been broken by a thin ledge of shale, stones, and tough, hillside grass. He looked up. If he stood to his full height and reached out his arms, Mattie might be able to reach the lip of earth from which he had fallen. Gingerly he began to test the ledge. Before he had time to stand, pebbles and soil scattered down from the pathway above.

Burns and the other men were closing in on him. Mattie eased his back against the wall of the gorge and edged his way, step by step towards the waterfall. He could hear his pursuers clearly. Their voices beat upon the air.

'Where? Where are they?'

'I don't know. The dogs are going wild. They must be close.'

Mattie could hear the dogs coughing and choking as they strained against their collars. Their paws scraped at the edge of the cliff. Mattie took shallow breaths, and moved shakily along the ledge. He reached a point where the entire ledge had fallen away into the water below. It was a jump of about a metre to the next part. Mattie's legs quivered under him. He thought his heart was about to burst through the wall of his chest. He sprang towards the other side of the gap. Scrambling desperately for his footing, Mattie steadied himself. He'd made it.

He was within spitting distance of the waterfall. Inside his head a voice was screaming: 'Run. Run. Run and never stop.' The clouds were racing across the azure sky, and in the racing clouds were faces, and in the wind were voices. Mattie's senses were spinning. He was slipping once more, slipping into a whirlpool of faces and voices. The faces were the faces of his mother, and Prav and Joanne. The voices were theirs too. It was as if he had one foot in their world and one foot in this world of fear and revolt. Home was just a few steps away. One last effort and he would be there, free from the men who were chasing him.

He couldn't move. He prayed for a miracle. Just an ounce more strength to carry him under the water and out of their sight. His legs failed him. The sounds and images of home faded. He was lost. This was the end. In place of the hazy, half-perceived sensations of home there suddenly appeared a face which was only too real.

Burns was there, standing immediately above him. The slave-master's men fanned out on either side of him.

Musket barrels pointed at Mattie's head.

'You!' exclaimed Burns. 'Where are they? Where are my Negroes?'

Mattie couldn't answer. Burns cocked the musket's trigger.

'I said, where are they?' His lip curled in an ugly sneer.

Mattie forced out the words: 'There is only me. It's my scent the dogs followed. The others are long gone. You'll never catch them and I'm glad.'

Burns looked at the dog-handler for confirmation of what the boy had said. The man nodded nervously, afraid of Burns' anger.

'A white boy who runs with Negroes. Nobody will miss one traitor,' said Burns. 'Did you see how my men died, boy? Now you will know what it feels like.'

Mattie closed his eyes.

The shot he heard caused him no pain. A shadow passed over him, followed by a rush of wind, then the sound of yelping.

Mattie opened his eyes to see Burns spreadeagled on a rock far below. In the water, two bloodhounds were struggling to the bank. One by one the men on the path dropped their muskets. Mattie heard the sound of them being collected.

'Now, jump!'

It was the voice of Brother No-one.

Mattie clung to a tussock of grass, as the overseers plummeted feet first into the pool fed by the waterfall.

Brother No-one reached out. 'Take my hand, Mattie.'

As he was hoisted onto the path, Mattie began to tremble and sob uncontrollably. He was panting with fear. Brother No-one held him for a second.

'Come with us,' he said. 'This place is still full of danger.'

Mattie raised his face to see Cuffee, Yambo and Adjaba. They were bearing captured muskets. Two armed men kept look-out.

Kota squatted on a fallen tree trunk. He grinned. 'So you can do magic. Did you fly?'

Mattie peered ruefully over the side and winced.

Cuffee said: 'There is plenty of time for this later. The soldiers have been seen. The musket shot will have alerted them. We have to go.'

'Is everyone safe?' Mattie asked anxiously.

'Yes,' said Cuffee. 'They are safe in the forest. The mountains are just two day's march away.'

Mattie rose unsteadily to his feet. As he did, he heard the sound of hooves on the stony floor in the gorge below. An officer on horseback was riding at the head of some twenty soldiers. One young soldier was helping Burns' men from the pool. 'They're all right, Sir,' he said, 'but this one's dead.' He was pointing at Burns.

Mattie followed the example of the slaves, slipping away quietly from the cliff's edge.

A shout came up from the floor of the gorge. 'Sir! I saw movement. Up there. I can't be certain, but I think it was a man.'

Brother No-one waved everyone through the bushes. 'Move! I'll try to stop them.'

Cuffee handed him his musket and some ammunition. Brother No-one knelt down and prepared to fire as the soldiers began to make their way up the side of the gorge. Mattie heard the crack of Brother No-one's musket as he hurried after the others.

Mattie paused a little way up the hillside. Adjaba glared at him. 'Come on, boy. We can't wait for Brother

98

No-one. He will find his way to our camp.'

'That's not why I stopped,' said Mattie. 'I know this place. I think I can find my way home. I can't come with you.'

Cuffee stared at him in disbelief. 'The soldiers are behind us. They may already have captured or killed Brother No-one. You must come with me.'

Mattie shook his head. 'This isn't my home.'

Cuffee gestured to one of his men to look out for the soldiers.

'Whatever is calling you is strong. Live a good life, Mattie.' He squeezed the boy's arm. 'Mattie?'

'Yes?'

'Try to tell your people how it was. Tell them who we were and how we lived. Most of all, tell them that we dreamed of living as a free people.'

Mattie nodded. His voice might let him down. Then Kota stood before him, attempting a joke: 'And I thought you were going to teach me how to fly!' Kota's joke sounded to Mattie like the saddest thing in the world.

The look-out returned and said: 'The soldiers are coming. I can't see Brother No-one anywhere.'

Cuffee led the way up to the top of the hill. Mattie watched as the band vanished from sight. Only Kota remained. He smiled briefly then raced after the others. At the top of the hill he paused and waved. Then he, too, vanished from sight.

Mattie pushed his way through the undergrowth which masked the cave's entrance, then listened. He couldn't hear the soldiers. He began to wade through the shallow water, and peered into the gloom. At last he found the passage into the depths of the cave. 'You're not home yet, Mattie lad,' he thought, 'What if there is no way back?'

A voice shattered the silence. 'We lost them Sir, and the dogs are in no condition to follow them into the woods.'

'Search the woods,' shouted another voice. 'We can't go back empty-handed. Our good ladies would never rest in their beds.'

'Ladies!' said another. '*I* won't rest in my bed if they all fight like the one on the hillside.'

Mattie heard the boots of at least one soldier on the stone floor of the cave. The entrance had been discovered.

Mattie moved into the darkness. Soon, to his relief, he felt ice-cold water running over his face. 'Almost there,' he murmured to himself.

He felt for the opening in the darkness, but what he touched was neither water nor rock. It was a man's hand. The fingers closed on his wrist.

'I've got one, Sir!'

Mattie cried out. He struggled, but was held fast in the soldier's grip. With his other hand he could feel the sides of the crevice. How could he be so close to freedom and yet so far? Then he felt as if the opening too was pulling him. Yes, the rock itself was breathing. It was a living thing. Suddenly, Mattie heard its voice, the voice of the rock.

'You're not alone, Mattie.'

The soldier's vice-like grip loosened on Mattie's hand. He sensed the man's body being lifted into the darkness.

'Brother No-one? Is it you? Are you alive?' whispered Mattie hoarsely.

The voice replied: 'They can't kill a dead man, can they?' The words echoed around the cave.

Mattie thought he felt fingers touch his face, then the presence was gone. He gasped: 'Brother No-one. Brother No-one! Was it you? Were you real?'

A moment later he heard another voice, then another. More soldiers were coming.

Mattie hurled himself into the darkness. It yielded and he was falling, part of a slow, sighing wind. Around him, he could feel things passing. He heard a voice, a stranger's voice, but not threatening. It spoke clearly, as if addressing a great gathering:

'I am a slave. I tell my story to let the people know the truth; and I hope they will never give up and will call loud till all the blacks be free and slavery ended for evermore.'

Mattie heard a cry in the distance: 'Freedom now!' He felt a blast of flame and heard the cane fields crackling as they burned. Then he heard the crackling again, but this time it was different. It was not cane which was burning. There was a huge crash like a roof falling in.

At last, Mattie knelt on solid ground, gazing up at the shattered, fire-blackened rafters of Heywood House. He was back.

# CHAPTER TWELVE

# Return

Dust motes shifted and spiralled in the shafts of sunlight which pierced the gloom inside Heywood House. Mattie would normally have been unnerved by the dim and haunted surroundings. Now they gave him more pleasure than anything he could imagine. He was relieved and surprised that the house was empty and decaying. He fell in love with every derelict timber and brick in the place. He felt like yelling: 'Is anybody there?' but feared there might be an answer. The ghost of old Samuel Heywood might just be lurking in some dark corner.

'Leave well alone, Mattie lad,' he thought.

Mattie stood up and dusted himself off. At his feet he saw something familiar. It was Burns' conch shell. Mattie picked it up. He turned the pink and white shell over and over in his hands, feeling every ridge and line.

He smiled to himself.

He ran his hands over the dirty, cobwebbed wall where the painting once hung. The wall was hard, solid, impenetrable. He searched the floor for more evidence of his passage into that other world. There was none.

He lifted the conch shell to his lips and blew on it. At first he failed to produce a sound. After a couple more tries he managed a thin, piercing note which echoed eerily in the empty building.

In the silence that followed, he suddenly heard something. There was somebody else in the house. He stepped carefully over the rubbish which littered the floor. Even that was welcome; coke cans, crisp packets, plastic cups, the throw-away things of his own time. All the time he walked he listened for that other presence.

Easing open the door, Mattie slipped out onto the landing. The great staircase had long since fallen in. Somebody had leaned a timber against the remains of the landing to climb up. It rested precariously at Mattie's feet. Mattie's eyes ran over the scene in front of him. The only light here filtered through the fire-blasted roof. The windows were boarded-up. Then he heard a whimper, followed by scratching. Mattie tested the timber then half-slid, half-jumped into what had been the hallway. He picked his way through even more litter, stopping from time to time to read an item from a yellowed newspaper. He read the dates; every one of the papers was from the late nineteen eighties. Yes, he was back.

Mattie wandered down the hall. He tried to discover, in the skeleton of the shattered building, the great house which had been erected by the labour of generations of slaves. He could find little trace. Only the dimensions remained the same. The life had gone out of the place, and with it the terrible power it once exerted.

The sound came again, this time more distinct. It was coming from the other side of the front door. With a couple of kicks, he loosened the panel which covered the doorway, and stepped out into broad sunlight. There, in front of him, was a labrador dog wagging its tail for all it was worth.

Mattie knelt down and rubbed the dog's neck. 'Hello fellow. So it was you making all that noise, was it? Where are you from then?'

The dog had a name tag attached to its collar. It read: 'My name is Goldie. I live at Gatley Cottage.' There was also a phone number.

'I wonder who lives at Gatley Cottage,' Mattie said.

'I do,' said a woman's voice.

Mattie started and looked up to see a grey-haired woman in her sixties. He realized that he might be trespassing. 'Is this private property?' he asked. 'I didn't think.'

'Don't worry. It isn't worth anything in its present state. Few people come here now. Just me and Goldie, and the odd vandal. You're not a vandal, are you?'

'No.'

'Good,' said the woman. Then she added: 'You look as if you've been in the wars.'

Mattie inspected himself. She wasn't kidding. His clothes were creased and misshapen, even though they were clean. Adjaba had done that right, anyway! As for his hands, they were filthy.

'Did you see any ghosts?' the woman asked.

'Ghosts?'

'They say the place is haunted. I've never seen anything of course, and I've been coming here ever since I was a girl. I saw the fire, you know.'

'Fire?' Mattie had thought the woman a bit strange at first, but now he was interested.

'Yes, Heywood House burned down in 1933. I was ten years old at the time, about your age I suppose. The funny thing is, it burned down on the anniversary of the abolition of slavery, 1833. It wasn't just the year which was the same. It was the day too. Oh, silly me, I should have told you the most important part of the story.'

'The house was built on the profits of slavery,' said Mattie.

'Why, that's right.' The woman was surprised. 'How did you know that?'

'Oh, you'd never believe me.' said Mattie.

He noticed his bike, still leaning against the wall of the house. He found the idea of a bike being left unchained for days and not stolen almost as strange as the story of how the house burned down. He sat on his bike and turned to say goodbye to the woman: 'Keep believing in those ghosts, missus. You never know when you might see one.' He cycled off down the drive, leaving behind a very bemused old lady.

As he turned out of the drive and onto the main road Mattie glanced back. The house had disappeared from view. He looked at his watch, more out of habit than expection. One thirty-seven. *One thirty-seven!* Mattie shook his head and looked again. The display changed. One thirty-eight. Typical! His watch had decided to work now!

It wasn't worth worrying about. There were more important things to worry about than a boy-proof wristwatch which had just taken its annual holiday. Mattie knew the police must be scouring the city for him. He pictured his mother sitting by the phone, and snatching up the receiver each time it rang. Mattie rode hard down the road. At last he came across a call-box.

'Please don't let it be broken,' he thought. He put his only ten pence coin into the slot and waited impatiently. He half expected his mum to tell him how Joanne and the others had been beaten within an inch of their lives a couple of days ago in a confrontation at the Fleapit.

He heard his mum's voice: 'Hello, Colette Jones speaking.'

'Mum, it's me. I know you must have been worried, but I couldn't help it. I fell backwards through time, and got involved in this slave revolt. I'd never have got back but for Brother No-one. He saved my life, twice ...'

Colette Jones was used to her son's romancing, but this was a bit rich even for a boy of Mattie's imagination. She might have accepted some tale about a Yamaha which could break the sound barrier, but time travel!

'Mattie,' she said, 'will you slow down? What *are* you talking about? Why aren't you at school?'

Mattie glimpsed the time changing to one fifty on his watch. 'Mum, what day is it?' he asked.

'What day! It's the same day as when you left home this morning. Are you quite all right?'

The pips went. 'Thank goodness for that,' thought Mattie.

'I've no more money, Mum. See you –'

The line went dead.

'– soon.'

Mattie replaced the receiver. The same day! Then there was still time to put things right. He could still get to the Fleapit that night. He rode steadily home. There was no hurry now. Mattie enjoyed the commonplace sights he thought he'd never see again; ice-cream vans, bus shelters, skateboards, advertising hoardings. As he rode along Broadway he saw old Tommy. Tommy was there outside the supermarket rain or shine, proclaiming the end of the world. Mattie pulled up next to him.

'How are you doing, Tom? World ended yet?'

'It's no laughing matter, son.'

'What does your sign say today, Tommy?' asked Mattie. He inspected the sign: 'The answer is Jesus.'

'Fair enough,' said Mattie, 'but what was the question?'

'Cheeky young dog,' said Tommy as Mattie set off again, but he was smiling.

Mattie entered the square in front of the flats. 'Same old flats,' he thought. A net curtain twitched. 'Same old Nosy Reilly, too.' Mattie waved to Nosy Reilly. He saw the old guy turn bright red.

He hoisted his bike onto his shoulder and climbed the stairs three at a time. He rang the bell. His mum let him in and set about cross-examining him there and then.

'Come on, spit it out. Why were you skiving off school, and what was that nonsense on the phone?'

'Oh that,' said Mattie, 'a slip of the tongue.'

'You'll have to do better than that, son.'

'Sun spots?' bleated Mattie. 'Midsummer madness?'

Mum let the phone call go. She was more concerned about him bunking off school. She'd already button-holed his friend Pat Casson about it on his way home from school, and knew about the trouble in the yard.

Mattie managed to get through his explanation without a single flippant remark. He told his mother about Tony Doran and Pravin, and the scene in the playground. He took care not to mention the Fleapit that night. If Mum thought he was going to be involved in a fight, she would ground him for certain.

'I don't feel very proud of myself,' said Mattie. 'I should have stuck up for Pravin.'

'I think you're right,' agreed Mum, 'but don't worry about running away. We all get scared sometimes.'

'What if I had stood up to Tony Doran, though? What if there'd been a fight? You're always telling me to keep clear of fights.'

'Avoid trouble if you can, but sometimes you have to risk trouble to stand up for what you believe in.'

Mattie smiled. 'I'm glad you said that. I've come to the same conclusion myself.'

'With no help from Miss Smartypants?' asked Mum. She meant Joanne.

'Well, maybe a little,' admitted Mattie.

It was just then that Mum noticed the state of Mattie's clothes.

'Mattie Jones! Where on earth have you been?'

'Hell and back, Mum. Hell and back.'

Mum went into the kitchen to start the tea, muttering: 'Ask a silly question.' Mattie pulled the conch shell out of his jacket. Poor Mum. It was all a bit too much to take in.

Mattie's mother remained puzzled by her son's behaviour. Why was he glued to the news? Why was he reading the newspaper, the TV guide, even the calendar over and over again?

By the seventh time he checked the date with her, she felt like throttling him. 'Yes, Mattie. It *is* June 8th. It was June 7th yesterday. It's June 9th tomorrow. It was June 8th this morning. It was still June 8th this afternoon. It is June 8th now and it will be June 8th all evening until midnight. ALL RIGHT?'

Yes, it was all right. It was definitely all right.

Mattie left Mum in the kitchen, cursing the ageing microwave. He closed the living-room door and carried the phone as far down the hall as he could. He phoned Macca. Macca's name wasn't Mac-anything, but he lived on MacDonald hamburgers. He phoned Pat Casson. 'The dog' was a bit miffed about being grilled by Mrs Jones but he agreed that Tony Doran needed sorting out, and said he'd try to round up a couple of people. Finally, Mattie phoned Joanne. Before he had a chance to speak, she started to bend his ear: 'What got into you, Mattie Jones? Mrs Carroll went mad at me. I don't see why I should carry the can when you get a rush of blood to the head.'

'Can I get a word in edgeways, Megamouth?'

There was a shocked silence at the other end of the phone.

'Charming!'

'Sorry, but I had to get you to listen to me somehow. Look, I will be there tonight. I've phoned a few people. I think they'll come. I don't know about you but my bottle's gone. Oh, Mum's coming. I'll have to go. See you later.'

Mattie hung up.

Mum called: 'Was that the phone?'

'Yes, somebody trying to sell you new kitchen units.'

'Chance would be a fine thing.'

'That's what I said,' quipped Mattie, brightly. He had never, but never carried off a white lie quite that professionally.

Mum gave Mattie a funny look as he set about his tea like a wild thing.

'Mattie! Don't bolt your food.'

Mattie paused.

'It's very flattering to my cooking, but it's only pasty

and chips.'

'Only pasty and chips! Have you ever eaten salt-fish and rice two days running?'

'No,' replied Mum. 'And neither have you.'

'Well, that just proves my point, doesn't it?' said Mattie.

Colette Jones stared at her son. Midsummer madness? Maybe that was it.

After tea, Mattie was like a cat on hot bricks, pacing the floor and checking the time on his watch with his Mum's.

She was at the end of her tether. 'What *is* going on, Matt? First it's the date, then it's the time. You're driving me nuts.'

Mattie shrugged his shoulders. He decided it would be better if he headed for the Fleapit and killed a little time down there. If he stayed in the flat he would give himself away.

'I'm just off out for an hour, Mum. I said I'd call in at Joanne's.'

'Take care, Mattie. Don't be late back. It's a school day tomorrow. A *full* school day.'

# CHAPTER THIRTEEN

## Settling Accounts

If you knew Mattie, you would instantly recognize him as he wandered along the dry, dusty streets. He had four gears, did Mattie Jones. He usually went through life in first, which was day-dreaming. He changed up easily into second, which was rapid-fire talk. He often changed up again, into third, which was helpless, infectious giggles. This gear, like second, was only ever employed in the company of friends. Fourth was his response to any sort of bullying or cruelty: Run away!

On the evening of Monday, 8 June at a quarter to six, Mattie was definitely in first gear, with the distinct possibility of slipping into fourth if he was to run into Tony Doran and his mates while he was on his own.

Mattie looked down past the decrepit flats and the warehouses. Between the drab walls he could see the river. It had been full of ships, this river, in years gone by; trading vessels, warships, slavers. It was empty now. It wasn't the river of the Empire any more. It was Mattie's river, his silent witness.

'I'm back,' thought Mattie, looking at the glistening waters, 'back in my own time.'

The past had closed its door on him. It was already hard to summon up the faces of Adjaba and Kota, of Brother No-one and Cuffee; and it was getting harder all the time. It was as if a mist was rolling in between Mattie and the world of the Heywood Plantation. Mattie wanted to see them, talk to them, touch them. It was with them that, for the first time in his life, he had known exactly where he stood. He had taken sides easily, unprompted by anyone or anything but his own conscience. It had been instinctive. He had seen what was wrong. He had done what was right. Here, now, things became difficult again. He knew fighting wasn't the answer. Wouldn't it just provoke Doran and Co., and besides, wasn't there a better way?

If Mattie had met himself coming the other way he would have given himself a good thump. He might not know how to win the battle which faced him, but he knew he wasn't going to run away from it.

'After all I've been through how can I dither?' he thought.

He hung around the window of a record shop for a couple of minutes, noting the titles of the tapes he couldn't afford. He heard a familiar sound. It was the engine of a trail bike, tuned to perfection. Mattie turned the corner to see the two bikers from outside school tinkering with their bikes outside a tower block.

'Hi, kid. Aren't you the one we see every dinner-time, looking at the bikes. Would you like to take a proper look?'

'Can I?' asked Mattie.

The two youths were proud of their bikes. They were in their element guiding Mattie around the controls and treating him to tales of their many tumbles and scrapes.

'I could top your stories,' thought Mattie, 'but you'd never believe me.'

'What was all that about in the playground earlier on?' one of the bikers asked him. 'I saw Tony Doran mouthing off as usual.'

'Do you know Tony?' asked Mattie.

'I know Joe Clarke and his family better, but I've met Tony Doran all right. He's a born trouble-maker. I'd keep out of his way, if I were you.'

'I wish it was that easy,' said Mattie, 'I've tried keeping out of his way, but he and his mates just keep coming after me. A mate of mine is the wrong colour as far as they're concerned.'

'Up to their old tricks, are they?' the biker said. 'They put stickers all over our fence one morning. I had murder with them over it.'

'What were they putting stickers on your fence for?' asked Mattie.

'Jacko goes out with Carol Mason. They call him a nigger-lover,' said the other biker.

'Carol Mason,' said Mattie. 'Has she got a brother called Jimmy?'

'That's right,' said Jacko, 'do you know him?'

'Yes, I'm seeing him down the Fleapit. Tony Doran challenged him to a fight.'

'Did he now?' said Jacko. 'Take care of yourself... What's your name, anyway?'

'I'm Mattie, Mattie Jones.'

'I'm Phil Jackson, but you can call me Jacko. This

is Dixie. I'm just off to pick Carol up. I think she'll be interested in what you've told us.'

'Come on, Jacko,' said Dixie. 'It's gone six.'

'Gone six!' gasped Mattie, 'I've got to go. See you.'

'Maybe sooner than you think,' said Jacko, but Mattie didn't hear. He was running as fast as his legs could carry him in the direction of the Fleapit.

Mattie reached the walkway which led down to the car park in front of the Fleapit. From his vantage point on the iron-railed walkway, he looked down on the bar-rack-like building. It had been a cinema, then a Bingo Hall. Now it was a drab, useless hulk, fit only to have footballs hammered against its walls.

There was a new addition to the graffiti which covered them.

It read: 'White Power.'

Standing in the car park with their backs to their latest handiwork were Tony Doran, Joe Clarke, Ian Williams and four others. Each one of them was just the type to pick a fight. Pravin and Jimmy were there, accompanied by three of Jimmy's mates, and by Joanne. Good old Joanne, always true to her word, and always on time. Mattie weighed up the balance of forces. It wasn't too good. Doran's group were at home at the Fleapit. It matched their characters: wretched, neglected, and threatening. There were more of them and they were older and more used to fighting.

Joe Clarke stepped forward and started pushing Pravin in the chest. Pravin stood his ground. Joe took to giving him little slaps on the cheek, each one harder than the last. Suddenly, Pravin reacted. He grabbed Joe's wrist and swung him off balance. Ian Williams made a move, but found Jimmy Mason blocking his path. Mattie watched the skirmish with mounting anxiety. 'We're on a hiding to nothing,' he told himself.

Tony Doran was in his element: 'One Paki, four nignogs, and a girl. I'm shaking in my boots. You're going to get what you deserve this time, Mason. You should have kept your nose out of our business. Let the Paki fight his own battles.'

Mattie ran down the steps of the walkway to the car park. He shouted: 'It's my battle too, Tony.'

'And ours.'

The voice belonged to Pat Casson. Macca was with him. So were Terry and Graham Davis, Phil Vernon and Teresa Bentley.

'Where have you been?' Joanne asked Mattie. She spoke angrily but quietly. She didn't want Tony to hear.

'I got held up,' confessed Mattie, 'I don't know about this lot.'

'Oh, we got here ten minutes ago,' said Pat. 'We've been watching you from over there.'

Joanne set her jaw. 'You mean you let us go through this? I'll have the runs all night because of it!'

'It was Macca's idea,' said Pat. 'He said he fancied leading the Seventh Cavalry.'

'The Seventh Cavalry were massacred at the Little Big Horn,' said Joanne.

'Oh,' said Macca. 'Not a very good comparison, was it?'

Tony Doran whispered something to Joe Clarke. Joe took off round the corner of the Fleapit.

'I don't like the look of this,' said Jimmy. 'We've definitely got more people now, and they don't seem bothered.'

Four more of Mattie's classmates turned up to support Pravin. Still Tony smirked in a way which told everyone present that he wasn't finished yet. A moment later, Mattie saw why. Joe came back round the corner with his big brother Billy and two other older lads. All three were sixteen or seventeen years old. Billy and his two friends sported enamel Union Jack badges.

'We're going to get battered,' said Pat Casson.

Billy didn't seem to be in any hurry to 'batter' anyone. He was really enjoying the discomfort of the younger children. Some of them had turned up out of a sense of duty, others out of curiosity. Either way, they were no match for the three teenagers.

'Don't tell me this is the pathetic bunch who've been giving you bother, Joe.' He gave Jimmy Mason a sharp dig in the stomach which made the younger boy wince. 'You wouldn't hurt a fly, would you Jimmy? There you are, Tony. I think Jimmy wants to apologize, don't you Jimmy?'

Pravin stepped between Jimmy and Billy. He said: 'Leave him alone. I'm the one this trouble is about. Talk to me if you've got anything to say.'

Billy's face contorted with hatred. 'You cheeky little get. I'll have to sort you out.' He threw a punch at Pravin who ducked and hit his attacker back, though without enough force to hurt his taller, stronger opponent.

Joe gripped Pravin's arms from behind. 'I'll keep hold of him for you Billy. Hit him.' He leered at the other children, who were watching with a dumb resentment. 'Anyone want to stop us?'

Mattie tried, but was knocked to the ground by a slap from Billy. He wiped his nose. It was bleeding.

Tony joined in the taunts. 'Anyone else? There's plenty more where that came from? Anyone else fancy themselves?'

Mattie picked himself up in time to see Billy head-butt Pravin just above the nose. The younger boy's head snapped back. Mattie was white with powerless anger.

There was nothing he could do to prevent his friend's humiliation.

Mattie could do nothing, but Joanne could.

She dug her carefully nurtured nails into Billy's neck. He let out a shrill scream of pain.

'You rotten little bitch!'

Pravin took advantage of Billy's discomfort and dug his elbow into Joe's stomach. Then he spun round and struck Joe full in the face.

The sudden exchange of blows ended the phoney war. Punches and kicks landed. Mattie knew his friends had little chance. Though they outnumbered Doran's group, the three teenagers more than made up what they lacked in numbers. Macca and one of Jimmy's friends already sat winded on the ground. Billy was dragging Joanne over to one side by her hair. She was crying. Mattie had never seen her so upset, but she was hurt and frightened.

Then Billy shouted: 'I've had enough of this. You kids are going to get a lesson you won't forget.'

'Will they, Billy? Who from?'

The voice was accompanied by the sound of motor bike engines. Jacko and Dixie skidded their bikes to a halt in front of Billy. Riding pillion on Jacko's bike was a black girl dressed for a night out.

'This has got nothing to do with you, Jacko,' said Billy. He didn't look so confident any more.

'Hasn't it? You've been having a go at Carol's little brother, and Mattie here is a friend of ours. I think this disagreement can be sorted out without any help from us, don't you? You're a big boy now. What are you doing picking on kids from Junior School?'

Billy exchanged glances with his two friends. The two sides were even now. It was stalemate.

Jacko said: 'Your move Billy. Do you think it's worth the trouble?'

Jimmy Mason looked a bit worried, but not by the other side. He was glancing nervously at his older sister. Billy also looked worried. He scowled at Joe. He hadn't expected this turn of events.

Joanne took the initiative. She stepped up to Billy and said: 'Well, you were tough enough when it was just me. Isn't it time you cleared off and took your racist mates with you?'

Billy made as if to raise his hand but thought better of it.

Mattie spoke directly to Tony Doran: 'It's over, Tony. Tell them to go home. Your bullying will only work if we allow it to. I think that from now on we will be sticking together, don't you, Pravin? We know whose side we're on.'

Pravin didn't say a word. He didn't need to. The expression on his face said it all.

Jimmy Mason forgot his sister for a second and joined in: 'Nobody's afraid of you any more, Tony. There are more of us than there are of you, and Joe's brother won't be in school to help you. You'd better face it. Pravin is here to stay.'

Tony looked around. Most of his mates had slipped away already. He spat on the floor in a parting gesture and walked away.

Billy grabbed Joe's arm and dragged him away. He could be heard telling his younger brother to: 'find out what you're getting me into next time.'

Mattie watched the opposition break up. He approached Jacko and Dixie.

'Thanks. We'd have been battered if you hadn't turned up.'

'Forget it,' said Jacko. 'We evened things up a bit, that's all. It was down to you kids how you sorted it out.' He twisted the throttle on his bike. 'Ready, Carol? The film starts in twenty minutes.'

Carol was giving Jimmy a right telling off. He was shuffling his feet and looking away. She finally softened and ended by saying: 'Still. They were a bunch of creeps. Don't worry. I won't tell Mum and Dad. Just keep out of trouble, that's all.'

The bikes rode away.

Mattie joined his friends. Joanne was inspecting her damaged finger nails.

Jimmy said: 'Forget your nails, girl. Think what you must have done to his neck!'

Joanne smiled, then gave Mattie a long look. 'What's come over you then, Mattie? I thought you didn't want to know.'

Mattie didn't like being reminded of the way he had behaved that morning. But that was in the past. He knew it wouldn't happen again.

Pravin said: 'It hardly matters now, does it? You were all here when I needed you. It's horrible when you think you're on your own.'

'Don't I know it,' muttered Mattie, then, as if to demonstrate the new Mattie, he pointed at the White Power slogan on the wall and said:

'I'm bringing a can of whitewash down tomorrow to paint out that muck. Anybody else coming?'

'You're on,' said Joanne. There were nods from Pravin and Jimmy.

'Anyway, I'm going to get off,' said Jimmy. 'Is anybody coming my way?'

Joanne and Pravin joined him. The others waved and took their own ways home. Joanne turned to Mattie.

'Aren't you coming?'

'It's all right,' said Mattie, 'I wouldn't mind being on my own for a while.'

Mattie walked in the direction of the waterfront. He felt at ease. His step was light. He belonged here, by these waters which had seen so much. He thought of Samuel Heywood's ships which had sailed down the river and out to sea on their terrible quest. He thought of those who had profited from the trade in human souls, and of those who had raised their voices against it.

Dusk was gathering over the grey waters of the river. The reddening sun hung low in the sky. Mattie unzipped his jacket and produced the conch shell. He ran his hand over it, and smiled. He cast his eyes across the river. Just for a moment he thought he saw a sailing ship in the hazy mist in the distance. He looked again. It was gone. Mattie checked that nobody was watching him, then raised his hand and said goodbye to his friends down the centuries.

# Author's Note

The present-day events described in this book are set in the great city where I live and work, Liverpool.

Why Liverpool? Many other cities contributed to the evils of the slave trade, but none more so than Liverpool, the capital city of British slavery.

A few facts make this clear;

Liverpool's net proceeds from the 'African trade' in the peak years of 1783–98 were £12,294,116. That is £7.50 profit per slave.

For every five slave ships built in Britain, two were built in Liverpool dockyards.

Of Liverpool's mayors, 26 were slave merchants, or the close relatives of slave merchants.